STRONG
WINDS
FROM
NOWHERE

STRONG WINDS FROM NOWHERE

THE INITIATION OF THE ONE

A NOVEL

RONIT GALAPO

HAY HOUSE

Carlsbad, California • New York City • London • Sydney
Johannesburg • Vancouver • Hong Kong • New Delhi

Copyright © 2004, 2014 by Ronit Galapo

Published and distributed in the United States by: Hay House, Inc.: www.hay house.com® • *Published and distributed in Australia by:* Hay House Australia Pty. Ltd.: www.hayhouse.com.au • *Published and distributed in the United Kingdom by:* Hay House UK, Ltd.: www.hayhouse.co.uk • *Published and distributed in the Republic of South Africa by:* Hay House SA (Pty), Ltd.: www.hayhouse.co.za • *Distributed in Canada by:* Raincoast Books: www.raincoast.com • *Published in India by:* Hay House Publishers India: www.hayhouse.co.in

Cover design: Janus René Andersen

All rights reserved. No part of this book may be reproduced by any mechanical, photographic, or electronic process, or in the form of a phonographic recording; nor may it be stored in a retrieval system, transmitted, or otherwise be copied for public or private use—other than for "fair use" as brief quotations embodied in articles and reviews—without prior written permission of the publisher.

This is a work of fiction. Names, characters, places, and incidents are the product of the author's imagination or are used fictitiously. Any resemblance to actual events or locales, or persons living or deceased, is strictly coincidental.

Tradepaper ISBN: 978-1-4019-4136-9

TO JOSHUA

CONTENTS

PROLOGUE

She was born on a dark night with a single cry, welcomed by the first dawn of a new spring. It was as if she was born to decipher the kingdom of darkness and bring it to light. On these very first morning rays she was marked, and from then on, this destiny of hers would follow her, each step, each heartbeat, each deed.

Her body was tiny and fresh. Yet in her eyes you could see all the sighs, all the cries, all the wrinkles. In her eyes you could see the sharp power of a knife. She was so tiny, so young, but her eyes couldn't hide her secret: that she was born old.

I, Ceyon, was her guardian, her teacher. But she surpassed me. I saw her in her utmost moments and was filled with enormous wonder and great respect.

I would like to tell you her story. Years ago my vanity wouldn't have allowed me to do so. Yes, vanity can darken one's eyes and twist one's heart so that the sight of a brave spirit can appear as too bright and too beautiful. But I have learned my lessons, and it is part of my legacy to tell you her story, rather than mine.

You may wonder how I could know all that happened. Some of the things she told me herself. Some, I had seen and witnessed. And some, I have my own ways to know.

All you are about to hear is as it truly was.

PART I

THOSE
ENDLESS
MEADOWS OF
INNOCENCE

1. TASHA

The First Day of Spring

Tasha was born in the spring. The leaves had dared to burst out and be green again. Grass covered the valleys like a magnificent blanket. You could see lovely colors of red and yellow. You could smell the blossoms, you could hear the birds, you could taste the fresh water and sense the warmth of the sun. It was a celebration. A sensual celebration. Everything evoked Life. Spring was her cradle. Nature had given her a glorious welcome.

She was born in the small, secluded village of Ingram. Years before, it had been an oasis, but the blessing had started to fade away. The people were farmers and quite poor. You could see some sheep, some cows, but mostly crops. The people hated the harsh beating of the summer sun and the unbearable bite of the winter. For those born in the summer or the winter, their lives didn't count for much. Their future was sealed. They were used as slaves.

Tasha was born on the first day of spring. One may wonder what might have happened if she'd been born a day before. Life is quite elusive. But, nevertheless, she was not born a day before. She was born in the spring.

Tasha's parents were simple people, hard workers. She was their fourth child, and it seemed as if she was just another one in the chain of survival. But then, her parents named her Tasha, which meant, "The one who reaches the ocean." For the people of this village, the ocean was not merely a vast expanse of water. It was considered the end of the world. And for one to reach the ocean required a great deal of bravery and creativity. It was a name never given to a girl before.

Tasha's parents didn't think about this when they named her. It was as if they couldn't help it; their inner instinct was stronger than they were. So Tasha it was.

The people in the village mocked them for naming their daughter something so grand, so impossible. But they had too many worries to take care of and couldn't care about a name. Yet this name, and this first day of spring, would give this vibrant baby all the ingredients she needed to reach "the end of the world."

Of course Tasha didn't know all these things—she was just a baby. But from then on, her voyage had begun. She would have to reach the ocean, no matter what.

2. FEAR

Go for the Ocean

Tasha was four years old when her mother died. Although she got affection from both of her parents, her father was mostly aloof. He worked hard and didn't talk much. Tasha's mother was gentle as well as strong, and Tasha felt safe next to her. She was only four, and she had already tasted the death of someone so dear to her.

The burial was quick. The man who was in charge said a blessing, and that was all. But Tasha felt she couldn't leave the grave without giving her own blessing. She asked to speak, to say her words. The man told her that children shouldn't speak at times such as these, so she must be silent.

But again she asked, "Please, let me say my words. I can see my mother, and she asks me, 'What about your blessing, my dear child?' I don't want to disappoint her."

And the man said, "Oh child, you are full of imagination. What will become of you? You think you see your mother because you can't let her go. But she is dead. You must accept it. You can talk to me, to your father, or to your brothers, but you can't talk to your mother. Do you understand that, child?"

Tasha looked at him and saw fear in his eyes. She saw great fear of death, but she didn't say a word.

That night, she put on her coat and silently walked out to her mother's grave.

"Dear mother," she said, "I can see you flying, light as a feather. The sight of you is so real, yet I can't touch you. I would like to touch you once more, just once more. Today I saw great fear in a man's eyes. Your eyes are so at peace, and I know that you are safe. Mother, I love you."

And her mother responded, "My dear Tasha, in your life, you will see fear; and you will see anger, hate, and anxiety. But if you are able to just see those things without feeling them, you will be safe. See the fear, but don't let it touch you. My beautiful little Tasha, I must go. I'll be with you even if you don't know it. Go now, Tasha. Go to your life; go for the ocean. No matter what, don't forget that. The ocean is waiting for you. Be blessed, my child, be blessed."

Tasha waved good-bye. She made her way home and never looked back again.

3. INGRAM

Too Beautiful, Too Bright

By the age of ten, Tasha had become a beautiful girl. She was so beautiful that people would feel an ache when they looked at her. The villagers were so used to shabby, dull colors, to rough heat and shivering cold, that Tasha's beauty was too much for them, and it made her a stranger. Tasha herself didn't know what she looked like. There were no mirrors in the village. Even though everyone knew your appearance, you did not. This could be a blessing or a curse. In Tasha's case, it was both.

When Ceyon first saw Tasha in the village years ago, he knew that this child was going to be beautiful. Her eyes were so deep and dark. In them, he saw the deepest well he had ever seen. He knew that this girl was born for a different journey.

Ceyon didn't have a family. He was raised to be a Shohonk. The Shohonks were people whose journey was to see beyond that which meets the eye. In order to achieve clear sight, they took upon themselves the commitment to never become attached to anything, for attachment causes blindness. After years of initiation, they could live wherever they wanted, but they couldn't raise families of their own.

Ceyon's story had been a secret to the people of Ingram. One day he had appeared in Ingram and since then he had brought dignity and common sense to the village. Sometimes people tried to figure out who he was, where he had come from. But because of hard labor and stressful times, no one had the spare time to look for the answers. As the years passed by, their appreciation of him overcame their curiosity.

In her childhood Tasha hadn't seen Ceyon much, but she knew that the people in the village had great respect for him and found him trustworthy. And in a place like Ingram, to be found worthy of trust meant a lot.

In Tasha's tenth year, spring didn't come. Winter lingered, hardening the ground, and all the crops withered and died. Everything was washed with a dark gray. The people of the village were very tense and angry. They cursed their gods, wondering what they had done for the angels to have deserted them. They started to look for the reason. They were hard workers, so it couldn't have been their laziness. They were poor, so it couldn't have been their greed. They were ugly, so it couldn't have been their vanity.

And then, in a meeting, the elders suddenly remembered that not all of them were ugly. They remembered Tasha, who was taller and more graceful than they were. They remembered the day she had been born, when their eyes had been washed by green, red, and yellow colors. They remembered that such beauty had never repeated itself. And so, the elders concluded that the day when Tasha was born, the gods had opened the doors of beauty to the village, but Tasha had taken it all. She took the beauty from the crops, the leaves, the flowers, and the rivers; and she left a shabby village behind, with shabby people, shabby houses, shabby crops, and shabby rivers. So they made a decision: Tasha must die. And upon her death, all her beauty would be poured on the village of Ingram, and luck would touch them again.

But then Teo, the oldest man in the village, remembered that the day Tasha was born was the first day of spring.

So he said, "Hear me now. We have forgotten that Tasha was born in the spring. Therefore, she is sacred, and no one can touch her."

You could hear the displeasure, although it was unspoken. But Teo had the final say, and no one would dare oppose him.

Then he continued, "It is decided. Tasha is to be banished from the village. Tomorrow will be her last day. Someone must go with her, and never abandon her. Who will take her away?"

Ceyon, who had been in the meeting, saw the fear and anger in the people's eyes. He knew that Tasha couldn't stay there, not even for one more day. He also knew that Tasha was born for a different journey, and needed someone whom she could trust and feel safe with.

So he stepped forward and said, "I will take Tasha away." Then he paused for a moment and continued, "I will watch over her and take good care of her. Tomorrow at first dawn, I will take her away to her unknown destiny."

The elders whispered among themselves. Ceyon was a kind of angel for the village, and it seemed that they didn't want him to leave.

Like the other elders, Teo didn't like this either. But he saw that Ceyon had already made his decision, so he said, "So shall it be."

Before dawn Ceyon woke Tasha. He told her to be quiet and come with him.

"Where are we going?" Tasha asked him.

"We can't speak now, we must go," Ceyon replied. "You must trust me."

"I want to say good-bye to my father and to my brothers."

And Ceyon said, "We don't have time. Don't say too much. Tell them that you must leave, but don't say good-bye."

It took some time. Ceyon was waiting for her. He had wanted them to leave at once, but he knew that he couldn't take Tasha without her consent.

After a while, Tasha stood in front of him and said, "I am ready. If we must go, let's go now." She didn't ask Ceyon for a reason. She just stood there and was ready to go, as if she had understood the urgency of the moment.

Ceyon looked at her. The fragile body and the immense strength in her eyes filled him with awe. *She is special,* he said to himself.

Then he said, "Let's go, Tasha."

With some small bundles, they headed toward the open horizon of the desert. Ceyon, a man in his forties, and Tasha, a ten-year-old girl, were going to the vast Nowhere. Tasha waved good-bye to the village of Ingram. She gave her hand to Ceyon, and they quietly walked away.

Some of Ingram's people said that on that day there was a marvelous sunrise. They had never seen such a sunrise before, and they never saw one as spectacular after that.

4. THE GREAT WOLF

Some Potatoes and an Orange

It was their first day together. Tasha was very quiet, as if she were in mourning, as if she knew she would never see her village again. She hadn't said a word, and it was almost noontime. Ceyon looked at the girl with great wonder. She didn't act like a little girl. She was not childlike at all. Ceyon hadn't said a word either. He held Tasha's hand, but he let her lead the way. He felt her grasp and through it, he could sense tenderness and determination blended together.

Tasha hadn't taken much with her, only her coat and some dates to eat. She hadn't planned anything. Ceyon had just taken some provisions with him and some water, trusting Mother Nature would be benevolent.

Suddenly, Tasha stopped and said to Ceyon, "We must stop here."

Although it was sudden, Ceyon didn't object. He knew that, when it came to senses and inner forces, nothing was sudden. It just appeared at the right time.

He stopped walking and asked Tasha, "What shall we do now?"

And Tasha said, "We must wait."

There was no shelter, no shade. It was springtime, but the sun showed no mercy. It was like a summer sun, strong and direct, as if the seasons were confused, moving from unbearable winter to harsh summer, with no pause, with no kind of transition. Yet the sun didn't seem to bother Tasha. Nothing bothered her. She was calm and peaceful. When Ceyon looked at her, he saw that the big wells of her eyes were not as dark as they used to be. Light had entered her world, and she had begun to blossom. Spring had touched her in her deepest soul.

How can I serve this child? he asked himself. *She is only ten, and yet she is so strong. She is only ten, and she is so old. How can I serve her?*

Ceyon sat next to Tasha, and although it was already noon, he didn't look for food. He just sat next to her. From time to time Tasha looked at him, but in her eyes there were no questions. She didn't ask for anything. She just gazed at him as if she didn't see him at all.

It started to get cold. Tasha put on her coat, but she didn't move. Ceyon didn't say a word. He watched her, curious to see what her next step would be.

The night came. Stars hung over the land like shiny gemstones. It became quite cold. Still, Tasha didn't move, didn't say a word, and didn't fall asleep. She was so alive, so vibrant.

At first dawn, she suddenly stood up and said, "We must go now."

A few minutes later, they continued along the desert trails, without a single word.

At noontime Tasha said, "Now we must eat."

She took her dates from her bundle and gave some to Ceyon: two for him and two for her. They ate the dates very slowly. Then Ceyon gave her some water, and when the meal was completed, Tasha said, "We must go on. We can't stay here."

And Ceyon said to himself, *She knows so many things. Yet she isn't aware that almost no one else knows what she knows.*

She was young, yet so bright. She knew how to cope with harsh weather and hunger. She understood the code of timing, without the need to follow the hands of time. She simply knew these things. She sensed them. No one had taught her. Ceyon knew that for a Shohonk to reach this stage, it usually took years of initiation. Merely a day had passed, and she already knew all of that.

They walked along and encountered the night, but Tasha kept walking. Suddenly, they heard a cry. It was the cry of a wolf. Tasha changed course and went directly toward the source of the cry. Ceyon knew that it was the cry of a wounded wolf, and that a wounded wolf could show her no mercy. But he didn't say a word. He didn't warn her because he also knew that it was for her to discover the secrets of life, and he was there for her.

It was a bright night, so they could see quite far into the distance. The cry became stronger and stronger, and Tasha seemed to become taller and taller. Ceyon couldn't sense fear in her, but he didn't know if this lack of fear was due to her full awareness or to the naïvety of childhood. He didn't say a word. He followed her as she led the way.

When she approached the wolf, she saw its wounds, and suddenly, she began to speak to the wolf in an odd combination of syllables. There were no words there, but Ceyon understood what she said.

He heard her say, "Dear wolf, your pack has run too far away to hear you. I know you are young, and I know you want your mother. Although she is not here, she *is* here, for that is the nature of mothers. They are always with us. You are wasting your power on self-pity. If you really want to meet your mother again, heal yourself. All of us know how to heal ourselves, and so must you. I can't heal you. I have no magic spell or medicine. Heal yourself, dear wolf, and stop feeling pity for yourself. You are not wretched. You are the Great Wolf. Don't forget that. You are the Great Wolf."

She waved good-bye and went on her way. The wolf stopped crying, and a serene silence spread its unspoken words over the dark desert.

Ceyon felt great wonder. In order to communicate with nature, years of training were usually necessary. But she somehow already knew how to do it.

How can I serve this child, he asked himself. *How can I serve her?*

They walked all night long. Yet in the morning, Ceyon could not discern a trace of tiredness or sleepiness on Tasha's face. He was curious to see what she would do about her next meal. After all, she must eat and drink from time to time.

Then Tasha said to him, "Let's find something to eat. I'll go to the east, and you go to the west. After a hundred steps both of us will find some food. We must walk the hundred steps in full in order to find it. Let's do it now." She turned to the east and started counting her steps. Ceyon turned west and did the same.

After a while, they both came back. Ceyon asked her, "What did you bring, child?"

Tasha opened her hands, and he saw an orange.

"Where did you get it? There aren't any orange trees nearby."

"I think it was left by a wandering caravan. I felt the coals of a fire and they were still quite warm, as if they had just left the place. All I could find was this orange."

Ceyon looked at her and said, "I found some potatoes. Let's go light a fire, eat the potatoes, and after that, enjoy the orange."

Ceyon thought to himself, *How is it that Tasha brought this extraordinary fruit, the orange, and all I found was plain food, potatoes? Although nourishing, it was too plain.* But he didn't like this thought. A grain of jealousy had penetrated his world. He reminded himself that he was her guardian, and Tasha needed his strength and integrity.

It was a nice meal. Yet, later on, Ceyon was still carrying the impression of Tasha's orange compared to his plain brown potatoes. And for a moment, the orange was too "orange" for him. However, he was determined not to let this thought dominate him.

5. THE SHOHONKS

Beautiful Wasn't the Right Word

Although she was born in a village, life in the desert came naturally to Tasha. So did finding food, creating shelter, and talking to animals and plants. She was a part of Nature. Without much training or practice, she had become a virtuoso.

Ceyon was dazzled by her brightness and by her inner strength, and felt confused by this. He wondered if his own years of initiation had prepared him for the immense task of serving and protecting this special girl.

Then he reminded himself that Tasha was only a girl who had passed ten springs—and there was a lot for her to learn, to experience—and he had taken it upon himself to be there for her. He reminded himself of Teo's words, "Someone must take Tasha, and never abandon her." But as time passed, he sensed cracks within himself, and his determination to be a true guardian and resist envy was fading.

It is too much light, he said to himself. *How can one person embody so much light, so much beauty, so much strength?*

Ceyon was raised to be a Shohonk master. The Shohonks were people whose journey was to bring clear sight to the world. They were boys who were born with the ability to see beyond the veils of reality. The masters of the Shohonks knew how to find these boys whose journey was to become Shohonks.

In order to gain clear sight, the boys had gone through a long and meticulous training. They were taught to avoid attachments and to transcend their emotions and desires. They learned to be one with nature. They were trained to cross time and space and to enter different dimensions to experience the complexity of life, of existence. When they reached the end of their training, the Shohonk men were on their own. They were sent to the four winds, where they had to find their way and place in the world.

When they left the training, after years of initiation, they were given a warning: "A Shohonk can never be a leader. The one who trains his eyes to see must keep those eyes fresh and clear. If you try to be a leader and rule over others, you will instantly lose your clear sight. Be wary of greed. Embrace who you are, and never try to be who you are not. Wherever you go, this warning will follow you."

Throughout his years of initiation, Ceyon was the closest person to his teacher. His abilities evoked wonder from everyone around him. Ceyon loved this. He loved applause though he knew this was vanity. It was a source of shame for him, yet he loved to be loved.

But when he looked at Tasha, when he looked into her eyes, he couldn't find a trace of this need for approval. Her inner strength was present—clear and innocent, yet at the same time very mature. She was so beautiful, although *beautiful* wasn't the right word. She was beyond words. Sometimes her sight was too bright, and he could feel an ache.

6. THE POWER OF THE WORD

The Book of Secrets

After walking along the desert trails for a few days, Ceyon told Tasha, "Let's make a place for us to stay. We will transform dry soil into fertile land without plow and oxen through the Power of the Word, the Power that can create inconceivable manifestations."

Then without a pause, he continued, "The Word is the creator."

Tasha looked at him as if asking, *What does this mean?*

"This is the opening sentence of the Power of the Word as it appears in *The Book of Secrets.*"

"*The Book of Secrets?*" Tasha asked with curiosity.

"The original *Book of Secrets* was written by the old sages and contains the secrets of how to operate in the Universe in a very powerful way."

"Can you tell me more about the Power of the Word?" Tasha asked.

"I can," Ceyon replied. "It might not be clear to you what these verses mean, but if you listen in silence, with no demand to understand, the words will open to you."

Ceyon paused for a while, and then started reciting, "The Word is the creator. It can create marvelous stones and awesome stars. It can create rivers and oceans, evergreen forests, and fragile flowers. It can create the winds and the birds, worms and big animals. It can create man. It can create God. It is God in a glorious manifestation.

"The Power of the Word is immense. Clear sight is needed. A fresh outlook is needed. A pure heart is needed. Without these three virtues, no one should use this Power. Beware of this Power, for it creates all that there is, for it creates it all."

Tasha listened closely, fascinated by the spell of the words and their rhythm. Ceyon spoke as if the text was dear to him and very much alive.

Then she asked, "Will you teach me how to use this Power?"

"I will teach you only what you need for our purposes," Ceyon replied. "As the book says, the Power of the Word is immense and so are its consequences. If used improperly, it can lead to destruction.

"When people's lives are at risk it could be exercised, but only by those who are well trained and fully understand the complex implications of using this Power. Therefore, don't use this Power to help others because you are not trained for that. Remember this, and you will be safe from its harsh consequences. Now let's turn the desert into a lively land."

Tasha was a quick learner. The land that surrounded them became green, trees filled with fruits, and fields overflowed with vegetables. The desert hadn't known such a blessing before. It knew how to be a desert, but Ceyon and Tasha had brought the land to its utmost manifestation. You could sense that the desert was proud. It had abandoned its old notions about being a desert. Ceyon and Tasha worked with the desert like a good teacher works with his pupils; and it was thankful, and poured its benevolence upon them, night and day, day and night.

Two cycles of springtime passed. Tasha was twelve, and the desert was now her home. Through those years, Ceyon and Tasha didn't meet many people, apart from a few wandering caravans. Tasha was growing up, becoming even more beautiful. Ceyon could still sense the ache, and he had tried to overcome it. He wanted to be a fine Shohonk for Tasha's sake and for his own sake, as well.

It was then that he decided to tell Tasha about his different journey. He wanted her to know, and he needed to remember it for himself.

"I was born to be a Shohonk," he told her. "The Shohonks are people who come for a different journey. They are born with the ability to see into the depth of existence. After years of initiation, this ability is taken to a form of art. Their vocation is to bring clear sight to the world."

"Is this how you gained your powers?" asked Tasha.

"Yes, it is."

For Tasha, the thought of people who came for a different journey sounded both mysterious and sublime, and curiosity led her to ask, "Am I a Shohonk, too?"

"No, you are not," Ceyon replied curtly, as if he didn't want to say more. Yet he continued, "Only males are born to this journey." Then he turned back to silence.

Tasha was excited by the new revelation about the Shohonks, but she respected Ceyon's silence and pushed her curiosity aside.

One day Ceyon said to Tasha, "We can stay here no longer."

Tasha didn't ask for a reason. She trusted him. Yet, when she looked around her and saw the beautiful green scenery in the midst of the desert, she felt sad.

"We turned this land into a fine place for us to live," Ceyon told her. "We have experienced the grace of Nature, but now is the right time to move on."

"I must say good-bye to Nature's grace," Tasha said.

"Don't say good-bye, Tasha. Say that you must go."

Tasha took some time for herself, and after a while she was ready. She stood in front of Ceyon and said, "If we must go, let's go now."

Ceyon looked at her and saw a glimpse of mourning in her eyes, yet he couldn't see a trace of fear or self-pity. *This child,* he said to himself, *is indeed special.*

They took some bundles and left all their hard work and the wonderful fruits of their labor behind them. Tasha waved good-bye, and she never looked back again.

7. JOSEPH

The Love That You See

After a few days, they saw a small village on the horizon. Ceyon looked at Tasha to see her reaction. It was her first time to enter a village since they had left Ingram. Yet Tasha was quiet and peaceful. They walked straight toward the village.

They reached the village by noon. The streets were empty. People were taking their rest. You could see some chickens, some horses, but there were no men or women to be seen. This village had a different presence, different from Ingram. In Ingram, no one rested in the middle of the day, and the streets were empty only at night.

Tasha walked ahead, as if she knew where she was going. Suddenly, she stopped in front of one of the houses and told Ceyon, "We must go into this house."

Ceyon didn't say a word. He stepped to the side and waved his hand, as if inviting Tasha to enter. Tasha knocked on the door, and a small boy opened the door and asked, "What do you want?"

"I would like to see your father," Tasha said.

"My father isn't here," the boy replied.

"What is your father's name?" asked Tasha.

"Joseph," the boy answered.

"Where can I find him?"

The boy laughed and said, "He is far from here. It's a long distance by foot."

"Can you tell me where I can find him?" Tasha asked again.

The boy stopped laughing and showed her the direction to go.

"He is working in the fields. He and his workers are there."

"Thank you," said Tasha, and she looked at Ceyon, "We must go there."

Tasha was determined in her walk. She didn't say anything. All she did was walk toward the fields, as if she knew that she would meet the boy's father. Ceyon didn't interfere with Tasha's way. He walked after her with a sense of adventure, and was curious to meet the boy's father as well.

They walked for hours, and then the fields were ahead of them. The wheat was quite high, and seemed ready to be harvested. They saw some people working, and Tasha walked toward them.

When she reached them, she asked, "Who is Joseph?"

The people looked at her with great surprise. They didn't understand what this girl was doing in their fields. Who was she?

A man stepped forward and said, "I am Joseph."

Tasha looked into his eyes as if she was looking for something, for a clue, a hint. They stood like this for a few moments. There was a heavy silence.

Suddenly, Tasha said, "We must talk, Joseph. We must talk."

"Who are you, and what do you want?" asked Joseph.

"We must talk, Joseph."

"About what? What do you want to talk about?"

All Tasha said was, "We must talk."

Joseph sensed he should ask no further. So he said to Tasha, "Where do you want us to talk?"

"In the left corner of the field," she said and started to walk toward the corner.

Joseph followed her. Ceyon began to follow as well.

But she said to him, "I'm sorry, Ceyon. I must talk to Joseph alone."

Ceyon respected her words and let them go.

When they reached the corner, they sat on the ground, and Tasha said, "You don't know who I am, but that's not important. Listen to my words. You must trust me. It's for your benefit and your family's benefit. Listen to me carefully, as it might help you."

Joseph saw this young girl and he heard the music, her music. She was self-assured, yet had no trace of vanity or pride. He couldn't refuse to hear her. Moreover, he wanted to hear her.

Then she said, "You have a lovely family, but your wife is sick. She has tried to give her best to you and to your children, but the illness has caught her. She doesn't want to die. She wants to live. I can hear her clearly. She is special, your wife. She doesn't feel sorry for herself. She doesn't blame God. All she wants is to live, and to enjoy your love.

"But you have become very serious. You forget to smile, you forget to hug. You are the only one who doesn't rest at noontime. You are running away from your family, feeling safe in the fields with your workers. You lose yourself in hard labor to forget the dark cloud in your life. Your wife hasn't died, yet you act like she is dead already. She is here, and she loves you.

"I have never met your wife, but I could hear her asking me to tell you this. Open your eyes, Joseph. You are losing your life. You are losing your children. You are not safe in the fields; you are safe at home.

"I don't know you. All I know is that your wife truly loves you. And when someone truly loves you, she knows all about you. She discovers your real treasures and sees your beauty. If you see love in the eyes of your beloved, it means that those eyes reflect you. Go and look into your wife's eyes, and if you can still see love, don't run away. Stay there and look into them, again and again. The love that you see in her eyes is you. It's you, Joseph. Now I must go."

Tasha got up, shook Joseph's hand, and walked away.

Joseph was amazed. His eyes filled with tears. Who was this girl? How could she know all these things?

"Wait!" he cried out. "Wait! What is your name?"

Tasha turned around. She gave him a big smile, waved her hand, and walked on.

Ceyon hadn't heard her words, but he sensed that the left corner of the field was filled with joy, as if angels had come to visit Earth. He also waved to Joseph and then followed Tasha.

Dear Tasha, he said to himself, *what will become of you? What will you become?*

8. THE POWER
OF INTENTION

No One Is Cursed

Ceyon and Tasha continued to move from one place to another. When Ceyon felt that Tasha had learned all there was for her to learn in a particular place, it was time to move on toward new lessons and new adventures.

Tasha met some people, but because she and Ceyon didn't live in the villages themselves, she didn't make friends. Yet she didn't feel that she needed *more,* and she didn't feel that she had *less.* She lived her life with full acceptance.

One could perceive this full acceptance as a state of being a slave with no free will. Ceyon saw around him the *slavehood* of humanity. All people, both master and slave, are in bondage, for it is the master who dwells inside that makes one a slave. There are many inner masters—the constant need for approval, the greed for more, the jealousy of other people's treasures. Tasha had no master inside her, so she was never a slave.

In Tasha's fifteenth spring, they settled for a time near a village called Litacca.

Although it was springtime, the weather was very cold, too cold, and suffering was everywhere. The sun was visible, but its warmth didn't reach the people. It was as if a transparent barrier existed between the sun and the earth.

Tasha herself was like a second sun. She was radiant, and her presence couldn't be ignored. Ceyon had taught her the secrets of the desert, the secrets of the forest, the secrets of the earth. Now, in her lessons, they had reached the secrets of the sky. And in the sky was this wonderful sun, but down below, there was no warmth, no mercy, no grace.

Tasha looked at the sun with Ceyon, and said, "I can maintain my body warmth, yet the people around me can't, and they are suffering. There must be a way to let the sun touch them. Do you know how to do it?"

"Tasha, you and I know that all is possible," Ceyon said. "But we must approach your request with modesty and with a fresh mind. Let me ask you some questions, and just answer them honestly.

"Do you think that the warmth doesn't reach the people because they are cursed?"

"In spite of the presence of suffering, no one is cursed," Tasha replied. "I look at the world, and the word *cursed* doesn't belong to it."

"Do you think that there is a barrier preventing the warmth from coming through?"

"There is a kind of barrier, but it isn't real. It was created by some force, and if we had the key to the force, the barrier would disappear at once. But I don't have the key."

"Tasha, do you want to find the key?"

There was silence. Ceyon didn't say a word, but simply looked at Tasha, and waited.

Finally, she said, "Yes. I want to find the key."

"Why did you take time to answer?" Ceyon asked.

"It's a great responsibility to answer this question."

"My last question, Tasha, is this: Who are you?"

Tasha looked into his eyes and said, "I don't know. All I know is that I want to find the key. It's too cold here. I can cope with it, but for the villagers it is probably unbearable by now."

Ceyon knew that he could rely on Tasha to tell her own truth. He knew that she wouldn't try to hide her intentions, and that she wouldn't say anything just to seem more wise or beautiful than she was. She didn't seek love. It seemed that she was love.

"There is a key," Ceyon said, "but we must use it carefully. We don't want to control the sun. However, we can show people how to keep their warmth and help them regain their life force."

"Wouldn't it be simpler to control the sun?" Tasha asked. "Why can't we remove the barrier directly?"

"If someone tells you, 'I can give you the key to the sun, or I can give you the key to help people keep their bodily warmth,' choose the people. If you choose the sun, many will be dependent on you. But if you give people the key, you will teach them a great lesson. From then on, when the warmth of the sun seems remote, each of them will have the key to break this barrier, this unreal barrier."

Tasha looked at Ceyon. She loved him for his honesty and wisdom, and felt that she could trust him.

Then she said, "Thank you. I will remember that."

And Ceyon knew she *would* remember.

Now was the time for Ceyon to reveal the Power of Intention. "Through this Power," Ceyon told Tasha, "people can create a new dimension within themselves, and exercise forces to influence their reality."

"The Power of Intention," he continued, "isn't about one's daily, everyday intentions. It's not about private intentions, either. It is about the intentions that merge the benefit of one with the benefit of all. Only then can the Power pour benevolence on individuals and the people as a whole."

"How can you know if your intentions include the benefit of all?" asked Tasha.

"Years of initiation and the ability to see into the depth of one's being are needed for that," answered Ceyon. And then he continued, "It's not a simple task at all, and it would never be."

"Intention seems like a soft and tender power," Tasha then said.

"Listen to how *The Book of Secrets* describes it," Ceyon replied, and then began to recite, "The Power of Intention is strong in its manifestations, and subtle in its application. Beware of attributing naïve virtues to this power, for it creates your reality and the reality of your children. The sum of all intentions will be the manifestation of the human existence."

Tasha loved to listen to Ceyon reciting verses from *The Book of Secrets*. Although the Power of Intention remained obscure, she could capture the spirit of it. It was clear to her that each of the Powers had its own strength and validity.

Then she said, "You taught me once about the Power of the Word and now it is the Power of Intention. Are there more powers?"

"Yes, there are," Ceyon said. "They are all part of *The Book of Secrets*."

"Are you going to teach me some more?"

"As I've told you," Ceyon said to her, "You were not born to be a Shohonk, Tasha. Yet, I'm willing to consider it along the way. For now, let's help the villagers."

Ceyon taught Tasha the secrets of the Power of Intention, and asked her to reveal to the villagers only what they needed to know to ease their suffering. And so she did, and they thanked her for that.

9. A DESPERATE CRY

Who Will Keep the Gates?

The remains of the cold winter melted away through the spring. But as Nature is sometimes fickle, summer arrived harshly. The heat was unbearable, and the houses of Litacca and the villages around it didn't offer good shelter. There were no rivers nearby, and a desperate cry was in the air.

Tasha felt the heat, and she knew that it could burst into a fire, an emotional fire. And she felt the danger. She told Ceyon about it, and asked for his advice.

She said to him, "We don't live in the villages, but that doesn't make us strangers to the people. I don't have friends among them, but I know them, and I can hear their cry. The cry is becoming stronger and stronger. And it's not the cry of just one person. It's a common cry. You can hear this cry even among the elders. I feel how the wisdom is fading away. Who will keep the gates?"

Ceyon saw that she truly cared. She heard the cry and couldn't ignore it.

So he told her, "The heat is not going to stop soon, and as you can sense, the people are close to the edge."

"That is why we can't wait," Tasha said. "Maybe I should ask to see the leaders of the villages."

"If you ask to meet with the leaders, you will be the messenger of bad tidings, and they may harm you."

"And what about talking to the villagers instead?" Tasha continued.

"You can't speak with them either. When they look at you, and they don't see even one drop of sweat, you'll be inhuman to them. From that point on, your life won't count for much.

"As you may understand, keeping the body from losing warmth is a different process from maintaining body temperature in extreme heat. Therefore, the villagers cannot use the key that you've given them. Nevertheless, we can still use the Power of Intention to help them, but only from a distance, and without meeting with them."

"It will take time to influence them through the Power of Intention," Tasha said, "and I don't think we have the time for that. When people feel strong heat, they are ready to burst out. I think this is the time to use the Power of the Word. You taught me that this Power can achieve immediate results, and it can be used to help people in the face of a crucial situation. I should talk to Solon, the leader of Litacca. He might be willing to exercise this Power."

"Tasha, you can't go," Ceyon said in a firm voice. "You might be in great danger, and your life is too sacred for that. I've never told you not to do anything. This is the first time. I'm asking you, and I'm warning you—don't go."

Tasha looked at him and said, "I am not saying good-bye. All I am saying is that I must go."

Then she turned around and started to walk away.

With a quick move, Ceyon stood in front of her.

Tasha stopped and gave him a sharp look.

"I'm sorry, Tasha, but for your safety, I can't let you go. You are not on your own yet. I took it upon myself to protect you," he said.

Tasha looked into his eyes and saw great fear. She had never seen such fear in Ceyon's eyes before, so she went back with him, and yet she knew that she still must go.

Later that night, Tasha went to find Solon. She didn't say a word to Ceyon. She just knew she had to do it. She respected Ceyon, she loved him, but her urge to go and seek help for the villagers was stronger.

10. SOLON

A River of Heat

Tasha left Ceyon sleeping and quietly slipped out into the night. The absence of stars made her path especially dark, but she relied on her senses.

Solon was the leader of Litacca, the largest village among all the villages in the area. He was admired for being as wise as the owl and as quick as the jaguar. He wasn't old, yet he was old enough to be respected. He wasn't young, yet he was agile and vigorous enough to be a powerful guardian. Tasha had met him before, and she felt that he might be willing to listen.

Ceyon had said that he could see traces of vanity in Solon's eyes and had warned Tasha that a person touched by vanity could not be trusted. Tasha remembered his warning, but hoped that Solon was stronger than his flaws. Although she trusted Ceyon, trusted his sight, she knew that Solon had a genuine chance to help his people, and she didn't want to give up on that.

Solon wasn't asleep. He sat outside his house. Tasha walked silently toward him, as if her footsteps might wake the village.

She stood in front of him and said, "Dear Solon, I know you see the things I see, and the picture is not good. But it's not enough for us just to see it. The one who really sees cannot remain indifferent. The heat is unbearable. And when the strong heat hits you, the inevitable outcome is terrifying.

"You must use the Power of the Word; otherwise, the roaring river of heat will sweep you all away."

Solon was quiet. Then he got up, looked at Tasha, and said, "The Power of the Word has not been used in the villages for sixty years. At that time, Noel, the leader of Litacca, used the Power of the Word to stop the villagers from fighting with each other. The days were hard then, and he wanted to lead the villages to a safer existence. He meant to do good, and in the end, the fighting was over. But the price was too high. Two villages were obliterated, and although the remaining villages lived in peace, Noel couldn't bear the high cost of this peace and killed himself. Since then, no one has dared to exercise the Power of the Word again. Noel left us a legacy: Don't play with powers if you don't fully know their consequences. You might achieve your will, but at what price?"

Tasha looked into Solon's eyes while he was speaking, and she saw that he had put a veil between them. She heard his story, but she didn't feel that he was being honest.

Then she said, "This story happened sixty years ago. Don't use this story as an excuse for not doing the right thing, right now."

Solon eyes darkened. "You're only a child," he said harshly. "You are not in a position to preach to me. I advise you to learn some modesty."

Tasha could sense his anger, so she softened her tone and said, "I might be young, but I can see. The Power of the Word exists to help people in times of need. Yes, the Power has its shadows, but I'm not willing to give up the Power just because of the shadows. What about you?"

Solon looked at her. She was beautiful, and her care was genuine and honest. Yet she was too young and had too much confidence.

So he said to her with a stiff voice, "Go back to where you belong. You are a stranger. You don't belong here. I have heard your words. Go now. You can't stay. Go."

Suddenly, Tasha saw great fear in his eyes. The harsh face and the stiff voice couldn't hide this fear. She remembered her mother's words. "You'll see fear and anger. You'll see hate and anxiety. If you are able to just see those things, without letting them touch you, you will be safe." So she gave a small bow and went away. She knew that she must now go to see Mira.

Mira wasn't a leader, but she was the oracle for all the leaders of the villages. They didn't do anything without her advice. After meeting with Solon, Tasha knew that Mira was the last chance. She reached Mira's house, but it was empty. She sat on the doorstep and waited for her.

Hours passed. Still, Mira didn't arrive. Many lives depended on one woman, and she wasn't there. Tasha knew that she couldn't stay too long. Although the people in the villages saw her from time to time, to them she was still a stranger. And now, alone, without Ceyon, she was even more vulnerable.

Suddenly, she saw someone coming toward her. She prayed that it was Mira, but it wasn't. It was Ceyon. She sensed his tension, but she knew that he wouldn't act on it. She could trust him for his dignity and honesty.

Ceyon looked at her and said, "Come along, Tasha, you can't stay here any longer. We must go."

Tasha didn't say a word. She stood up and went with him.

When they reached their place, Ceyon said to her, "I asked you not to go, and you decided to go anyway. You didn't dare to tell me; you just went. Don't do that again. You are not living alone. We live together. When you decided to go, you should have confronted me. It's easy to avoid confrontation. It's easy to not face reality. It's too easy to sneak off into the night. Yet the Power of the Word is more than saving the villagers. People with inner strength always speak. They don't run away from life. I'm not an obstacle in your life. I'm your teacher.

"I brought my presence in front of you. And from now on, no matter what, bring your presence in front of me. Otherwise, you are not living, you are merely functioning."

Tasha looked at him. She saw his concern and knew he was right. All she said was, "Thank you."

Then Ceyon said, "Mira came to warn us. Solon is planning to attack one of the villages to help his people release their despair and anger. Mira refused to give him her approval. She said Solon promised her not to attack, but she saw the destruction of the village in his eyes. And she saw you in his eyes. When you are in someone's eyes, you are in great danger. I know that you want to save people from their own dark spirits, but if the leaders are full of vanity, you must find a more subtle way to do so."

"Did Solon make the decision after he saw me?" Tasha asked.

"You will never know, Tasha," Ceyon replied. "And you'll have to live with it. You will just have to live with it."

11. THE POWER
OF THE HEART

Naked Heart and Bare Hands

Just before dawn, Ceyon and Tasha took their bundles and left Litacca. They couldn't stay. Their lives were in danger.

Tasha didn't know if she had interfered with the stream of time, if she had changed the course of events. Nevertheless, she decided to move on. She could not live in the past; otherwise, the past would haunt her, but she knew that she must learn the lessons it offered.

She looked at Ceyon and the tension in him was no longer in his eyes. But she couldn't read his heart.

Tasha was in her sixteenth year, and she had never yet created friendships with other people. She didn't feel lonely, but she was starting to feel an inner yearning to live among others. Although subtle, it was there. Ceyon noticed this, but they didn't talk about it. Ceyon didn't ask Tasha about the things she didn't want to talk about. In his own way, he made Tasha feel like she had her own private world, although everything was transparent to his eyes.

One day as they sat near a small stream, Tasha said to Ceyon, "I love you very much, but I also want to meet other people and live among them. We are wandering from place to place. And in many ways, I love our life. But I also want to be a friend. I want to make a friend."

Ceyon looked at her and said, "Tasha, do you feel strong enough to be a friend, to make a friend?"

Tasha smiled, "I don't know if I'm strong enough. I won't know until I try—and I truly want to try."

"What does *friendship* mean to you?"

And Tasha said, "I have only a vague feeling about that. I can give you a list of ideas, a list of words, but I know that it's a poor way to try to grasp what friendship is. All I can say is that I'm willing to come with an open heart to meet other people."

Ceyon paused for a moment. "A naked heart and bare hands . . ."

Tasha looked at him as if asking for the meaning of it.

"This is how *The Book of Secrets* captures the essence of what you describe as an open heart," Ceyon continued. "If you want to experience the Power of the Heart, which is the power of relationships, the book says that a naked heart and bare hands will be your only possessions."

"That is beautiful," Tasha said.

"It is, but experiencing it could hurt."

"Yet it could bring me great joy, too."

"Still, Tasha, it could be very painful," Ceyon said. *"The Book of Secrets* says that the mastery of the Power of the Heart is the most demanding. Do you know why?"

Tasha listened closely to Ceyon as he continued, "Because it asks a price, a personal price. You must give up your pride to gain the full abundance of this art."

"I'm willing to pay that price," Tasha said.

"It may sound simple, Tasha, but in moments of testing, you will experience unbearable feelings. Therefore, you must train yourself to open your heart. If you do it in one move, the book claims, it will be too overwhelming for your heart. Yet you can't do it in hesitation or fear, either."

"Have you experienced this Power for yourself?" Tasha asked him.

"We, the Shohonks, in order to maintain clear sight, took upon ourselves the commitment to never become attached to anything or anyone. We experience the Power of the Heart, but differently than others."

"So you won't show me how to use this Power?"

"I can't teach you how to use it. One has to discover the art of this Power. It is a lesson that you can learn only through your own experiences."

"Then I'm willing to experience it," Tasha said.

Ceyon closed his eyes and didn't say a word. Tasha watched him without saying anything either. She felt he wasn't at peace.

After a few moments, he opened his eyes and said, "If this is your will, so shall it be."

And all Tasha said was, "Thank you."

In the morning Ceyon said to her, "You have chosen to experience the Power of the Heart, which is one of the most difficult arts. Yet I see the strength of your will. Go on your way, Tasha, and I will follow you."

Tasha looked at him with much love and thanked him for his words. She knew that she was about to enter a different dimension. It was exciting, yet she also sensed fear within herself. But she didn't want to let fear distract her from her true wish for friendship.

12. LASSA

The Bright Side of Life

A few weeks later, leaving the threat of Solon far behind them, Ceyon and Tasha entered a big village called Lassa. It was just before noon, and the streets were full of life, busy with people, and with the hustle of carriages and horses. The atmosphere was welcoming.

They found an inn. It was the first time Tasha would live in a village since leaving Ingram. Ceyon paid the innkeeper and Tasha was impressed by the way he was handling life. She had never seen Ceyon making money. But somehow, he had always seemed to have what was needed. He was a magician in her eyes.

After they put their things in their rooms, Ceyon told Tasha that he preferred to stay at the inn, but that she could go out and explore and do whatever she liked.

Tasha walked down the streets of Lassa, absorbing the beauty of the village. She looked at the small houses, the green gardens, and let their beauty wash her eyes with joy and hope. If Ingram had been the dark side, here she met the bright side of life.

The people in the streets seemed gentle and nice. They looked at Tasha as if they couldn't ignore her. Tasha knew that others found her beautiful, but she didn't pay attention to it. She loved to see people, to watch them. She often found herself foreseeing their actions, as if she could read their minds and hearts.

She remembered Ceyon had once told her that when people are predictable in their decisions and actions, their free spirit isn't present, as free spirit is always unpredictable.

If people only knew how to be free, Tasha thought to herself.

When she returned to the inn, she asked Ceyon, "How can people free their spirits?"

"They must know first that they want to be free," he answered.

"Everyone wants to be free," she said.

"Deep inside, everyone wants it, but at the same time, most are afraid to be free."

So Tasha replied, "It should be the other way around. People should be afraid of *not* being free."

"In order to be a free spirit," Ceyon said, "you must change your habits. You must become unattached to things, to ideas. For you, this may seem a price worth paying. But for most, it's too demanding."

"But it *is* a price worth paying," Tasha insisted.

"Tasha, you cannot fall into the trap of knowing what is good for people and forgetting that they are human beings who make their own decisions.

"You are clever, but wisdom is where truth and love meet. Beware of truth without love, and beware of love without truth. Remember this, Tasha. You'll need it."

Tasha heard his voice and she heard the warning. And though the warning faded quickly, the impression remained. She knew that Ceyon gave her true love. No matter what she did, no matter what she said, he was always there for her.

13. THE KINGDOM

Too Deep to Cross

Winter came to Lassa. It was cold, and the days were bright. No dark clouds, no frozen fields. It was as if Nature showed its kindness to the people.

Tasha loved to work in the fields. She loved the fresh air and the people with whom she worked. She worked hard. All of them worked hard, but the people of Lassa didn't suffer from the disease that dwelled in Ingram. The people of Lassa put forth great effort, but they never felt cursed. They didn't have much money, but they never felt poor. They weren't beautiful, but they never felt ugly. They worked hard and took care of their small gardens, their small families, their small houses. But they didn't feel small at all.

Tasha loved this atmosphere. The people were kind to her, but she could sense that they kept a distance, as if she hadn't reached their hearts yet. Nevertheless, she liked the place and enjoyed to be among its people.

Ceyon didn't stay in Lassa all the time. He would go away for a few days, never saying where he went. Tasha never asked him about it. She knew it was for him to decide whether or not to tell her. She trusted him. She loved him. To her, he was the manifestation of a free spirit.

It was a rainy Tuesday, and Ceyon was away. Tasha was expecting him to return at the end of the week. She lived in the same inn that they had been staying at since they came to Lassa, and she felt at home there. But that day, she was restless. Even though the rain was getting stronger and stronger, she couldn't stay in her room. Tasha put on her coat and went outside.

Lia, the owner of the inn, advised her to stay indoors. "Be careful, Tasha. Although this rain seems full of grace, it can be quite dangerous. Stay in for a while, and let the rain subside. Then go and enjoy the fresh weather. The smell of the air after a good rain is the best."

"Thank you," Tasha said, but she still felt a strong urge to go out. "I know that it's raining quite hard, but I must go." And she walked outside into the rainy street.

The rain was so strong that she couldn't see the way. Tasha relied on her senses to lead her to where she must go. From time to time she stopped and found shelter. But soon she felt the urge and kept on walking.

She reached the gates of Lassa and passed them. She didn't feel fear, and although she was wet, she didn't feel cold. She knew how to use the Powers, and she used them wisely. She kept on walking. She crossed many fields. She didn't know where her feet were taking her—she didn't think about it, she just walked on and on.

Night fell and it became dark. And she walked and walked and walked. She felt vital. She was as fresh as if she hadn't walked at all. Lassa was far away by now.

The rain stopped, but mud was everywhere. Tasha reached a place from where she couldn't continue. The ground was too muddy to traverse. If she tried to cross it, she might sink. So she was standing there, in the middle of the night, alone. She didn't know what to do—Lassa was too far away, and the mud was too deep to cross.

Suddenly, she felt the cold. She had started to lose her inner warmth, and she couldn't warm herself. She was wet, cold, and alone. She didn't let fear touch her, but she knew that she wouldn't survive the night.

So she sat on the ground and asked for help. She prayed for Ceyon to come and help her. She was close to the edge, and she couldn't face it by herself. She needed help as she had never needed it before.

She talked with Ceyon, even though he wasn't there. She told him, "Dear Ceyon, I want to live. I've reached the edge. I can't go forward because it's too muddy. I can't go back because it's too far. I can't stay here because I'm losing my strength. All I can do is ask for your help. I'll learn my lesson. I am not trying to avoid this. But I must live in order to learn it. Without your help, I will die. Please come now. I pray for help."

The cold weather showed no mercy. Tasha felt herself losing her senses, and she fainted.

When she woke up, she found herself back in her room. She saw Ceyon's face and was filled with joy to see him. She couldn't speak. She was shivering. Ceyon didn't say a word. He just brought her his grace. She tried to ask questions. She tried to ask *how.*

But Ceyon said to her, "Go to sleep, Tasha. You need a long sleep. It's not a good time to talk. You are safe now."

Tasha fell asleep. She slept for a few days. In her sleep she dreamed that a beautiful bird had carried her on its back to a palace. She could sense the gentle wind on her face. She could sense the warmth of the bird. In the palace, she saw Ceyon. He was amorphous and untouchable. Tasha tried to hug him, but she couldn't. He was there, yet he wasn't.

She asked, "What has happened? Why can't I touch you?"

And she heard Ceyon say in a deep, frightening voice, "Welcome to my kingdom."

Tasha shivered. "What do you mean?"

And Ceyon, with a burst of laughter, replied, "Welcome to my kingdom."

Tasha looked around her, and she saw that the walls of the palace were made of water, the floor was transparent, and there was no ceiling above her. Tasha insisted, "Why is everything so unreal, so distorted?"

Ceyon didn't answer her question. He simply repeated, "Welcome to my kingdom," his voice roaring like thunder.

"Who are you?" she asked.

And the same sentence kept coming.

There was no mercy in the voice, neither was there love.

Suddenly, Tasha woke up, sweating and afraid. But then she saw Ceyon's face, and he was full of grace. She told Ceyon about her dream. And he said, "Don't trust dreams. Trust your feelings, Tasha."

Tasha didn't tell him that she was frightened, that she felt fear. All she said was, "Thank you, Ceyon, for saving me. I really wanted to live."

Ceyon looked at her and said, "It's still not a good time for us to talk. Sleep, Tasha, you are safe."

14. THE POWER
OF COMMAND

That Day

Tasha and Ceyon never spoke about what had happened *that day.* Ceyon didn't say anything about it, nor did Tasha ask. But she felt that on *that day* something had happened between her and Ceyon. She trusted him and knew that he was there for her. Deep in her heart, however, she felt that experience had been a turning point. Nevertheless, she decided to leave it aside and do whatever she could to regain her strength.

A few weeks passed, and Tasha still hadn't fully recovered. She was frail and weak, and mostly stayed in bed. When she slept, the dream of Ceyon came again and again, as if it were a warning. When Ceyon left for a while on one of his mysterious trips, Lia lovingly took care of her. She gave her water to drink and fruit to eat. She changed her bedding, opened the window when Tasha felt hot, and warmed the room when Tasha shivered. Lia had become, in a way, Tasha's family.

Lia was in her mid-forties. She was graceful in her appearance, in her walk, in her touch. She wasn't overly emotional, and yet she was always fully present. She told Tasha that in her youth, she had dreamed of an exciting life. But life's stream had taken her on a different course. She hadn't thought she would become the owner of a simple inn in a simple village, but she respected life as it was. She was a widow. Her husband had disappeared into the desert one day and never came back. She didn't have children. But she wasn't bitter. She trusted life. She didn't trust Ceyon, however. She never told Tasha this, but Ceyon sensed her distrust. From the first moment they entered the inn, Lia loved Tasha and didn't trust Ceyon.

One night, Tasha woke up startled from the haunting dream. Lia was there. She hugged her and told her that everything was all right. Tasha felt the need to tell Lia about her recurring dream.

Lia listened with full attention. She wasn't sure if it was just a dream or a sign of what was to come, but she didn't bring that up.

When Tasha finished describing the dream, she said, "I love Ceyon. I love him very much, and I can always trust his honesty. How can I rid myself of this haunting dream? I don't want to feel this way toward him."

Despite her lack of trust about Ceyon, Lia respected the love Tasha had for him. Thus, all she said was, "My dear Tasha, it was only a dream. You don't have control of your dreams. If you love Ceyon, don't be afraid. Your love will be there." She hugged Tasha, and wished her a warm goodnight.

Tasha was filled with love. When she looked into Lia's eyes, she saw dignity and honesty. She couldn't see a trace of fear. She couldn't sense any vanity. She thanked Nature for bringing Lia to her. Then, she drifted off to sleep.

But the dream didn't vanish. It kept on coming.

Tasha tried not to fall into a deep sleep, as if she could control the reappearance of the dream. Yet even if she slept only for a few moments, it was there: the bird, the palace, the elusive figure of Ceyon, the water walls, the transparent floor.

When Lia came to bring her food, Tasha told her that she couldn't stop the dream. "It comes again and again. Since *that day,* it never stops. It only becomes clearer and stronger. I can't tell this to Ceyon. I don't want to hurt him."

Lia listened to Tasha's words and asked, "What happened out there, in the middle of nowhere? How did you get back? Did Ceyon tell you what really took place?"

"Ceyon hasn't told me anything. We have never spoken about it. It's as if he doesn't want to hurt me," she replied.

"Dear child," said Lia, "maybe the key to the dream is there. You told me that you have some powers. Can you look into your past and see what happened?"

"Yes, I could do that, but I'm not allowed to. To look into the past, one must have the inner strength to face the temptation to change it. Sometimes the sight is so painful, you can't bear it. You need great inner strength to face the past without changing any events, without feeling the pain, the suffering, the loss. I haven't reached this stage yet."

"Who told you that you are not allowed to look upon your past?" Lia asked.

"Ceyon. He is my teacher, and I trust him. Ceyon says that when you deal with such powers, you must grasp the complexity of the many layers of existence."

"Tasha," said Lia, "I don't fully understand, but my simple instinct tells me that you are haunted by your past, rather than your dreams. If you want to wait to reach the right stage to look into your past, that is for you to decide. But I feel that this dream will keep coming until then. And it's a question, whether or not you can maintain your strength until that time.

"I understand that Ceyon is your teacher, and you have told me how much care and love he pours upon you. When I look at you though, I see a free spirit with no master to obey. I don't want you to go against Ceyon, but I also don't want you to go against yourself. It's your dream, Tasha. It's your reality, your life. It's for you to decide."

Tasha remembered Ceyon talking about the Power of Command. How it enabled one to gain a clear sight of the past or future.

"It is as if all your life will be there for you to see," he had said to her. "But if you are not ready, *The Book of Secrets* says, you could get stuck in one dimension, and it could lead to destruction, even if your intentions are good.

"I will tell you the secrets of this Power, but never use it without my guidance. When you've reached the right stage, only then can you use it."

She remembered his warning, but the dream was turning her life into a nightmare.

As the days passed, Tasha began feeling very confined in her room. She couldn't go out, she was too fragile. She couldn't stay in, because the dream was there. Again, she sensed she was close to the edge. But this time, she couldn't ask Ceyon for help.

She remembered that when she had sat there in the cold night, her first prayer had been for Ceyon's help, but she didn't feel the same now. She didn't feel that he could help her, and she didn't like this feeling. He was her teacher and was there for her. Yet no matter what she thought, no matter what she believed, she couldn't put this feeling aside.

Lia was like an angel who had appeared at the right time. Although she was attuned to her instincts and feelings, she didn't have the powers of Ceyon. Ceyon knew the right timing, and the right Power to use. Tasha didn't know what to do. She felt imprisoned. She felt trapped.

And the dream kept coming relentlessly. Again and again and again.

One morning, Tasha sat up in her bed and decided to look into her past. She asked that the gates of the Power of Command be closed if she was not allowed to see. But if it was permitted, she asked the gates to open for her. She sat in her bed, closed her eyes, and let herself enter the unknown.

Suddenly, without knocking, Ceyon was standing before her. Tasha couldn't hide her surprise. She saw tension in Ceyon's eyes and body, but she trusted him. He never let tension rule him. Yet she sensed fear.

"What are you doing, Tasha?"

"I'm praying for help. I can't get rid of my dream. It's haunting me," she answered.

"But what are you doing?" he asked again.

Tasha didn't say a word. At that moment she didn't see any grace or love in his presence. He was alert, too alert. She had never seen him in that state.

Yet when he looked at her again, his eyes softened, and he said, "I can see that you aren't feeling well. Why didn't you ask me to help you?"

"I didn't want to hurt or disappoint you."

"Tasha, never turn to the Power of Command without my consent. You must be fully guarded when you enter the realm of the past or the future. You can't enter this kingdom without my approval."

Tasha shivered when he said the word *kingdom.* It reminded her of the haunting dream, and the sound of this voice was the same. She didn't say a word or even look at Ceyon. She didn't want him to see her fear and shivering. She knew that she could hide her feelings, but her eyes couldn't hide her secrets.

"Be well, Tasha," Ceyon said, and left the room.

Tasha didn't enter the gates of the Power of Command that day. And the dream didn't disappear. She sensed that a struggle was yet to come, but she wasn't ready to face it.

15. LIA

Rust, Friction, and Noble Metal

This time, Ceyon stayed away longer than usual. By the third week, he sent Tasha a message saying that he wished her good health and trusted her wisdom.

A few months had now passed since *that day,* and Tasha still wasn't well. She was too weak to walk, too frail to come back to reality. Lia didn't like this at all and hovered over Tasha, tending to her every need. Lia knew that she couldn't go against Ceyon. She understood that if she tried, Tasha wouldn't cooperate. Tasha loved and trusted Ceyon, as if he were her only family, and she didn't want to take this from her.

But as the time passed, she saw the price. Tasha grew weaker and weaker. Although her spirit was firm and full of strength, her body was so fragile. Too fragile.

Lia couldn't understand why Ceyon, who had all the powers, didn't help her. Why wasn't he there?

Since the day Ceyon had appeared in Tasha's room and forbidden her to use the Power of Command, Tasha hadn't tried again. Yet Lia strongly felt that using this Power was the only chance for Tasha, but didn't know how to influence her. She knew that her loving care of Tasha was not enough.

Then, on a fine clear day, Lia decided to act. Tasha's condition continued to worsen, and Lia knew that she didn't have much time to live. Every day her health was deteriorating.

Once Tasha fell asleep, Lia went to Ceyon's room and began to look for a hint. If she could find out what had happened on *that day,* she could unveil this dark secret. So she looked through Ceyon's books and into his things. Suddenly, without any warning, Ceyon appeared in the room. Lia needed only a moment to regain her composure.

Then she heard Ceyon ask, "What are you doing in here?"

"I had decided to clean your room and wanted to surprise you. After all, you've been away for a few weeks, and I wanted to freshen up the room and open the windows."

Ceyon looked at her. Lia knew that he saw through her words, but she wasn't frightened at all. She wanted Tasha to live. She didn't care about Ceyon or his privacy.

"I don't need gestures of that kind," Ceyon said to her, and asked her to leave his room.

Lia did so, but she didn't hasten her pace. She walked out of the room slowly, upright, full of integrity. She was not a thief. She just wanted to help Tasha, and she was determined to do it. She was the only one who could.

After a short while, Ceyon came to visit Tasha. She was in her bed.

"Hello Tasha," he said to her. Yet Tasha was too weak to speak.

Despite her weakness, she radiated beauty. When people are sick and fragile, they often lose their spirit and become bitter, full of blame and self-pity. But not Tasha. When Ceyon looked into her eyes, he saw those endless meadows of innocence. He couldn't see a trace of anger or self-pity.

I know that she is safe and well protected, he said to himself, and then he thought, *Although weak, I can see in her this inner strength as if she is made from only one noble metal, like gold.*

Even in the eyes of his own master, he could at times see the rust, friction, and fusion of different sorts of metals. But he couldn't see this in Tasha's eyes.

Lia came into the room and saw Ceyon. She had caught him by surprise. He was so deep in his thoughts that he hadn't heard her coming, yet his appearance didn't reveal his feelings.

He looked at Tasha again and said to her, "Despite how it looks, I know you'll be well."

Tasha remained silent.

"You'll be well, Tasha."

Then he said good-bye to Lia, telling her that he must go. He didn't know when he would come back, but he would definitely return.

Lia heard the warning in his voice, but she didn't care about the risks. In spite of Ceyon's words to Tasha, she knew that Tasha's life was at stake, and she was the only one who could help her. She was her only friend at that moment.

16. CROSSING THE LINE

Remember Your Name

Lia had waited for the morning. She knew that she couldn't act at night, for in that profound silence, a good listener could hear your deepest thoughts.

The activities of the morning, the sounds of the people going to work, would serve as a kind of curtain. She didn't know if it would stop Ceyon from coming again, but she needed all the help she could get from the Universe. So she waited for the morning, and morning had come.

She went to Tasha's bed and woke her. Tasha was very weak and could hardly speak.

Lia said, "Tasha, you must choose life. Your life is too sacred to lose, and you are very close to the edge. I haven't tried to convince you; I haven't tried to force you to cross the line. But you don't have any other choice. You must look into your past and see what happened on *that day*.

"You must live, dear child, and you must live now. You don't have any other choice—you simply don't."

Lia saw the struggle in Tasha's eyes. It was a crucial moment. And she knew that there were only two answers: *yes* or *no,* which meant live or give up. Although she saw the conflict, Lia didn't feel pity for Tasha. She knew that Tasha hadn't loved yet, hadn't made the friends she wanted to make. She couldn't let Tasha fade away from the world without experiencing the wonderful friendships she desired so much.

When she saw that Tasha had fallen asleep again, she shook her and said, "Wake up, Tasha. I won't let you sleep. You must cross the line. I see you, and I see your strength. Remember your name. Your mother left you a legacy. 'Reach the ocean,' she told you. And now, I'm telling you the same. You haven't reached the ocean yet, so you can't give up."

Suddenly, she saw Tasha nod her head as if saying, *I'm going to see what happened there.* Tasha hadn't said a word, but Lia fully understood her eyes.

Tasha didn't move. She didn't change her position. She closed her eyes, but didn't fall asleep. Lia knew that she was crossing the line. All Lia did was hold Tasha's hand to let her know that she wasn't alone, that she was there for her, no matter what.

Lia noticed Tasha becoming restless. She knew that Tasha didn't like what she was seeing, perhaps that the picture she was viewing wasn't what she had thought it was. Her body began to shake. But Lia trusted Tasha to be brave enough to remain there and see what had happened. Lia tightened her grasp of Tasha's hand. She wouldn't let go. She wanted Tasha to know that reality was Lia's hand rather than the images she saw.

And after some time, Tasha opened her eyes, and Lia saw deep sadness in them. All Tasha said was, "He didn't help me. He didn't help me."

Lia hugged her. "Dearest Tasha," she said. "I know that you saw it all. You are so brave, and I'm proud of you. I can see you are hurting, but this is your chance to live again."

Lia didn't want her to speak and knew that a better time would come. Now was the time for Tasha to rest. Although she had slept a lot, it would be the first time that she could truly rest. The struggle was over. Even if it had hurt, it was better to see the truth. The truth always stops the struggle.

Over the following weeks, Tasha gained much strength and became alive again. But she wasn't the same. It was as if the experience had shattered her innocence. Ceyon had warned her that to live with an open and naked heart was going to be painful. He had also told her to beware of love without truth. And now, after seeing the truth, she knew that she must cling to it, in spite of how painful it was. Yes, she wanted to be a friend and she wanted to make a friend, but love without truth was not worthwhile. It could even corrupt your heart.

During those weeks Ceyon came to visit her twice. Tasha didn't know whether or not he knew she had used the Power of Command, but to her surprise, she didn't care. She showed much respect to Ceyon in his visits although her feelings toward him had changed, and she couldn't resist it.

She never told Lia what she saw. And Lia, who was happy to see Tasha regaining her strength, showed her own grace and modesty by never asking her.

Ceyon became a stranger, in a way, and Lia became her mother. She took care of Tasha and reminded her of her beauty, her force, and her name. Tasha loved Lia very much. She felt tremendous gratitude to her. After all, it was Lia who had saved her life, who urged her to see the truth. But at the same time seeing the truth was painful. So for Tasha, Lia was a strange combination of much love and much pain.

One fine morning, Lia saw Tasha packing her things. She understood that the time had come for Tasha to go into the unknown. Tasha was nearly seventeen, but she was a child in the sense that she didn't see the dark side of people. Lia knew Tasha's story was just beginning. She also knew that Tasha would have to face Ceyon again, but she didn't know when or how.

"Dear Lia," Tasha said, "I love you, but I must go, and I want to say good-bye."

Lia looked in Tasha's eyes. She saw that the ocean was already there.

She hugged Tasha and said, "I can't give you much, Tasha, but I want to tell you this: On your way to the ocean, stop in a town named Solla and look for Dara. She is a wonderful lady, and you should talk to her."

"I'll do that. I promise you."

Then Lia asked Tasha to wait and excused herself. When she came back, she handed Tasha a small bundle and said to her, "This money will give you the time you need to find your own way. Take it, and it will help keep you safe."

Tasha gave Lia a big hug, and for a while they stood there embraced—one woman, and another who was soon to be a woman, and the love was between them.

Tasha gathered her things and went out the door. She closed the door behind her, heading into the unknown once again. All she knew was that she must go, yet this time she chose to say good-bye.

PART II

IT WAS SWEET,
IT WAS BITTER,
IT WAS LIFE

17. BELLE

Different Place and Time

Summer had arrived. The valley was covered with blankets of green, filled with small rivers. It was fresh and alive, and so was Tasha. There were no remains of the haunting dream. There were no remains of the past.

Tasha was living in a town named Belle, which was larger than the villages she had known. The people of Belle seemed as if they simply lived there, without any sense of belonging.

Tasha could sense the loneliness among them, so she decided to create a place where people could meet and talk. She called the place "The Precious We."

Once they entered her place, she invited people to forget their pasts. "When you close the door behind you," she said, "you close the door to your past."

People accepted and embraced her, yet she remained a riddle for them. Who was she? Where did she come from?

Tasha didn't tell her story. She respected their curiosity, but she as well wished to leave her past behind. She wanted to be free from her past. She wanted to be free.

She was kind and friendly and knew people by their names, but she didn't make close friendships. Was it a matter of time, or was it something deeper than that? She didn't know.

One day, when she was sitting at her desk, a woman came in. This wasn't unusual, but something about this person was different. Although it was summertime, the woman's dress was made from thick cotton. She wore a hat that matched the dress, and she was draped in lace. She seemed to come from a different place and time. As Tasha approached her, she realized that she was a young lady, not the older woman she appeared to be.

"How can I help you?"

"I see that you don't remember me," the lady said.

Tasha looked at her carefully, recalling the pictures in her mind, but she couldn't find any picture of that lady in them. "I'm sorry. I don't recognize you. Who are you?"

"I'm sorry, too. If you don't remember me, I can't tell you another word."

"You must have me confused with someone else."

And the lady, agitated, said, "Do you think that one can confuse you with another? Is there another woman like you?"

She saw that the lady intended to leave. So she said to her, "Please, tell me your name."

The lady looked at her and said, "You forgot your past too quickly. You closed the door too soon. There is nothing wrong with letting go of the past, but your past is still alive, too alive. The valley is nice, but you don't belong here. You must go back to the desert and face your past. The moment you forgot who I am, you forgot who you are."

The lady turned and walked out, closing the door behind her. Tasha couldn't move. She heard the beating of her heart. Until that moment she felt that she had created a fresh life for herself. Belle was a hospitable town, and she had wanted to help people leave their pasts behind them. Now she realized that it was her own past that she was trying to forget. Who was this woman? Was this all a dream? Was it reality? Was it the nightmare returning?

18. SID

Some Riddles to Decipher

It was lovely that summer in the valley. Nevertheless, Tasha sensed a dark storm coming, one that she would have to face. She didn't know what it meant, but she knew that the storm would come.

She couldn't stay in the valley anymore. She couldn't stay in this summer. It had been a short, pleasant period, but it had come to its end. She must leave, and she must leave now. She left a good-bye note to the people she had met, took her things, and went toward the open arms of Nowhere again.

At the gates of the town, a man came to her and said, "You are doing the right thing."

He was young and had a strong presence.

Tasha had never seen this man before. But it seemed as if he knew her. She didn't know whether the wind had spread the word already about her leaving, or whether he simply knew her.

And the man said again, "You are doing the right thing."

Tasha looked into his eyes, trying to figure out who the speaker was. His voice was familiar, but she was certain that she hadn't seen him before.

"How do you know me?" she asked.

"All I know is that you are doing the right thing," he replied.

Tasha didn't say another word. She passed the gates, leaving the man behind her, and went toward the desert.

Tasha reached a village just before sunset. She didn't know its name. She didn't even know where she was. All she wanted was a room for the night and something to eat. She saw a big sign that said, "This is the hotel for you." So she walked inside.

It was small and plain. It looked clean, but there was no one there to welcome her.

Finally, a young boy appeared and asked, "Do you want a room?"

"Yes," she replied.

"My name is Sid. What's your name?"

"I'm pleased to meet you, Sid. I'm Tasha. Can you take me to my room?"

"My father will come soon," he said. "He'll show you to your room."

"Thank you," said Tasha.

The boy was friendly, and the hotel looked warm and welcoming. Yet Tasha sensed fear, but she didn't know why.

A few minutes later the father came. He was a bit drunk and in a good mood. He talked loudly, but seemed like a nice man.

When they reached Tasha's room, he said, "I wrote the sign outside for you. I knew you were coming."

"I didn't know that I was going to visit this village. How did *you* know?" asked Tasha.

The father laughed and said, "I know a lot of things. Enjoy your room. Don't be afraid. You are safe. Now have a rest." And he left.

Tasha felt the walls of a prison surrounding her. In one day, the lady, the man at the gates, the owner of the hotel—they all knew about her. But she didn't know who they were. She didn't understand what was going on.

Maybe Ceyon was right, she thought. *Maybe when I used the Power of Command, I got stuck in one dimension. Perhaps I'm in a prison and don't know it.*

She saw that a meal had been prepared for her, a warm, inviting meal. It was waiting for her on the table in her room. *There are some advantages to this situation,* she said to herself. *I'm hungry, and I'm going to enjoy this food.*

She was preparing to sleep when she heard a knock on her door.

"Who is it?" she asked.

"It's me, Sid. Please open the door."

She opened the door and invited him in.

"I'm too young to understand what's going on," he said. "I didn't know that you would be so beautiful or so nice."

"What do you know?" Tasha then asked.

"I don't know much," he replied.

Tasha hugged him and said, "Thank you, Sid. You must leave it to me. I have some powers, and I can take care of myself."

Sid's eyes widened. "What kind of powers do you have?"

"It doesn't matter. Trust me, I'll be fine. Go and have a nice sleep, and I'll see you tomorrow."

She sat on her bed and prayed for protection. She promised herself that she would do anything to set her heart free. But there were still some riddles to decipher, and she was determined to do so.

19. ELIJAH

Roads Traveled Only by Men

Tasha woke up startled, as if sensing that she was not alone in her room. It was dawn already, and the village was silent. Tasha had known many dawns in her life. They usually brought fresh vitality and new hope. But this dawn was different. It was heavy and dense, and she could sense a cry of despair. It wasn't a nightmare. It was her reality, and she didn't like it.

She didn't want to stay in the hotel any longer. She decided to move on.

When she silently left the hotel, she noticed that the sign wasn't there anymore. It was as if this village had been built only for her. There were just a few houses and nothing more. It seemed like a stage setting, rather than a real village. Was it real? Was it merely an illusion? She didn't know if she had crossed the line and lost touch with reality. The whole setting seemed surreal, so unreal.

She left the place with great relief and walked where her feet took her. She remembered the lady, who seemed to be from a different place and time. She thought about Sid and the man at the gates. She had seen them. They were real people. But everything was becoming so elusive, as if she had entered Ceyon's kingdom.

Everything was so real, and yet there was nothing for her to cling to, to rely on.

On her way, she saw large fields cultivated with great care. She decided to follow where they led.

When she reached the end of the fields, she was surprised to see a big house standing there alone. She had expected to find a village or a town. A lot of hands were needed to make those fields the way they were. She decided to see who lived in this house, who was the magician who knew how to work with barren soil without the help of many hands.

When she got closer to the house, it was smaller than it appeared. From a distance, it had looked almost like a castle, but it was a small, simple home.

She knocked on the front door. And as there was no reply, she knocked again. Then she sat on the doorstep and waited. Someone would eventually come, and she wanted to meet the person.

Suddenly, she saw a woman approaching the house. Tasha stood up to greet her. When looking at her, Tasha couldn't tell whether she was one person or many. She looked young, and then suddenly she looked old. She looked vital and alive, and then she looked tired and filled with great despair. Tasha hadn't seen a sight like this before.

Is she a part of the illusion? Tasha asked herself.

When the woman reached the house, she said to Tasha, "Please come in. Don't stay outside."

She didn't ask for Tasha's name, or question why she was there. She only invited her into the house.

"Don't be afraid," said the woman after they sat down. "I heard you last night. You asked for protection. I know that you want to be a free spirit, but you have a long way to go, and I can help you."

Tasha didn't know what to say. It was too overwhelming for her.

The woman said, "My name is Elijah."

"My name is—"

"I know," Elijah replied. "I know. You don't have to tell me."

"It seems that everyone knows more than me. What's going on? Is this real?"

"No, Tasha, it's not real, but it's your reality."

"I feel trapped. I can sense the walls of my prison. Everywhere I go, I meet people who know me, but I don't know them. Men and women I've never seen before. What's going on?"

"I'm sorry, but I can't tell you much," Elijah answered. "Yet I would like to tell you some other things that might help you. Did you see the fields around this house?"

"Yes. They are beautiful. Did you cultivate them with your own hands?"

"I did. This is my art, my work. I know how to cultivate seeds in a vast field of sand."

"This is a miracle," Tasha said. "You know how to create miracles."

"You did the same in the desert," Elijah said.

Tasha looked at her with great surprise. "Were you there?"

"You don't have to be in a certain place in order to be there," she replied.

Tasha looked at her, and suddenly, she understood. "You are a Shohonk, aren't you?"

And Elijah said, "Yes, I am."

"But how can that be? You are a woman, and the Shohonks are all men."

"My parents intervened with destiny by giving me a name that was never given to a girl before," Elijah said. "They fooled the gods. They fooled the Shohonk masters. My name changed my path. I am a woman who walks along roads traveled only by men. Your parents did the same to you. Your name marked your path."

Tasha was silent. Then she asked, "Do you know Ceyon?"

"Yes, I do."

Tasha didn't say another word. It was too much for her.

"You can stay for a while," Elijah said. Then she continued, "Look, Tasha, I can't save you from your journey. It's for you to live it. But now have a rest. You are safe."

Tasha remembered the father in the hotel, who had told her the same thing. The fields were real . . . but this woman, was she really a Shohonk? Tasha didn't have the strength to look into it, and she fell asleep.

When she woke up, it was already night. Elijah had lit a fire. It was warm and cozy, but Tasha sensed fear.

Tasha sat next to the fire. Elijah wasn't in the room. It was a small house indeed, not at all similar to a grand castle. But it was a nice house, a comfortable one.

Elijah came into the room and brought some food. "You must eat, Tasha. You must gain strength. You have a long way to go."

Tasha looked at her. She told her that she wasn't hungry.

"Even if you aren't hungry, eat the meal. You will need your strength."

"Thank you, Elijah. But I'm just not hungry."

Elijah was surprised. She knew that Tasha hadn't eaten anything. She looked at Tasha, saw her beauty, but couldn't discern what was behind her words. It was as if Tasha had put a veil between them.

"Tasha," said Elijah, "I don't want to hurt you. You don't have to eat if you don't want to. I'm not your enemy."

"I know, and I thank you," Tasha replied.

She didn't touch the food. She looked into the fire as if she were seeking a clue, a hint. Elijah watched Tasha, and Tasha sensed it.

After a while, Tasha said, "I must go now."

And Elijah replied, "Stay for the night. It's cold outside. Stay until first dawn, and then go wherever you want to go."

"Thank you, Elijah. But as you said, I have a long way to go, and I prefer to start now."

Elijah didn't respond, and Tasha left the warm and cozy house. She trusted Nature, but she didn't know if she could trust people.

It was a cold, dark night. The stars were hidden by the clouds.

Tasha found shelter under an old tree. She leaned against its trunk and felt safe, and then quickly fell asleep.

In her sleep, she heard a voice saying, "Dear Tasha, where are you going? Where are you going? Where are you going?"

The voice repeated itself again and again, as if it didn't expect Tasha to answer, as if there weren't answers to give.

Tasha asked sharply, "Who are you?"

The voice only said, "Where are you going?"

Tasha woke up from her sleep. The voices from outside and the voices from inside wouldn't let her rest, even for a few moments.

What's going on? she asked herself. *I have the powers to be a free spirit, yet I have become haunted.*

Then she heard her mother's voice, "Dear Tasha, go for the ocean. Go for the ocean, my child."

"Remember your name," Lia had told her. "Don't forget your name. The ocean is waiting for you."

Tasha sat in the midst of Nowhere. The ocean seemed so far away. Was it a fantasy? Was the ocean even real?

She waited for dawn, but she didn't know where to go. The lady, the man at the gates, the boy, Elijah. What was coming next? Although the desert around her was wide and open, she felt like a prisoner. She could sense walls surrounding her. She could dream about reaching the ocean, but the ocean vanished as soon as she opened her eyes.

She suddenly felt that she couldn't run away anymore. *I love Nature. I feel safe in the cradle of Nature,* she thought. *Yet I can't run away from people any longer. I didn't come on this journey to be safe. I'm willing to open my heart again. I will learn how to stay strong and firm in dire times, and I will face my prison. I must go. There are friends waiting for me. I must go now.*

20. THE TOWN

Same Words, Same Phrases

Tasha reached a town by nightfall. She saw some people in the streets. The weather was fresh and cool. She could sense autumn winds knocking gently at the door, as if they respected the people's desire for more days of summer.

Tasha stopped to eat. The woman in the restaurant didn't ask her anything. She simply brought her a good meal to recover her strength. Tasha didn't know it, but she looked very fragile, although her beauty was still so present.

After she ate, the woman came and said, "I see you are new in town."

"Yes, I am," Tasha replied.

Then the woman continued, "I'm Nula. Who are you?"

"My name is Tasha."

"I suppose you don't have anywhere to stay for the night," Nula said. "Although our house is not big and my kids are all around, I think it would be best for you to stay at my place."

Tasha told her that she appreciated it, and she would be pleased to stay with her.

"My house is next door," Nula said, "so you won't have to wait here until the restaurant closes. Come, I'll take you. It looks like you need a good sleep."

Tasha thanked her. But when she left the table, she saw something that caught her attention. At a nearby table, she saw a man who looked just like the one she had met at the gates of Belle. The resemblance was striking. It was as if they were twins.

She told Nula that she would be back in a moment, and she went to the man. She greeted him, and asked if he had a brother in the town of Belle.

"I don't know what you're talking about," he answered.

Tasha told him that she had seen a man who looked exactly like him in Belle.

He looked at her and all he said was, "Are you new in town?"

"Yes, I've just arrived," Tasha told him. "Nula, the lady from the restaurant, graciously offered me a place for the night."

The man said, "You are doing the right thing."

"How do you know that?"

"I just know that you are doing the right thing," he answered.

Tasha asked him for his name, but he said, "It's not the time to talk."

"Will I see you tomorrow?" she asked.

The man replied, "Go and get some sleep. You're safe."

It was becoming too much for Tasha. It was as if this man was a collection of the people she had met. She said good-bye and went with Nula. Nula was the only one who didn't know her, who didn't speak the same words as the others. She felt safe to go with her, to sleep in her home.

When Nula opened the door of the house, she stood in front of Tasha and said, "Welcome to my kingdom."

Tasha couldn't move. She couldn't say a word. She looked into Nula's eyes and saw innocence, rather than manipulation.

What's going on? she asked herself. It seemed that the language consisted of only a few words and sentences, and that was all. All the people she met kept using the same words, the same phrases. Nevertheless, she decided to stay at Nula's place, no matter what. She must confront her life. She must face what was there.

She remembered Ceyon's words about sneaking off at night, about how easy it is to avoid confrontation, about daring to face people. "Bring your presence in front of me," he told her. "Don't run away from life."

It was then that Tasha knew that she had to face Ceyon. Otherwise, she would be haunted by his words, his messengers, his spirit. But she had to prepare herself for that moment. She must become stronger in spirit and in heart. She must grow up and see things as they were. Right now, she was too fragile, too blind to face him.

She thanked Nula and went straight to bed. She didn't have a room to herself, but she didn't care. Her privacy wasn't important at that moment. Her privacy had already been invaded. People knew her. Dreams haunted her. She didn't want to be private. She wanted to be free.

She asked for help, and promised herself that she was going to devote her days and nights to being ready to face Ceyon. After all, her name was Tasha, and the ocean was waiting for her.

21. NULA

An Expert When It Comes to Food

Tasha woke up in the morning while everyone was still asleep. She took her things and went out silently. She knew she had to find a room in this town. She couldn't move again and again from one place to another. It didn't matter where she stayed. What mattered was her decision to face Ceyon. So instead of wandering from town to town, she would remain here. This town was as good as any other town. Tasha could stay here for a while, thanks to Lia and her benevolence.

She found a room in a small hotel. It was a bright room, with a window large enough to make the room seem bigger than it was. She felt hungry and decided to go have breakfast in Nula's restaurant.

Tasha entered the restaurant and found it filled with people. They seemed to know each other, like one big family. They looked at her as a stranger, and she sensed it.

Nula walked toward her with a big smile and said, "Good morning, Tasha."

"Good morning to you," Tasha answered. She told Nula about the pleasant room she had found, and thanked her for the night.

"You are welcome," Nula said. "Come, have a seat. It's breakfast time."

Tasha thanked her and sat down.

Then Nula said, "Dear Tasha, you are my guest from now on. Whenever you want to eat, this is your place. You don't have to pay. All you have to do is eat your meals with pleasure. You must build some strength, and I will be happy to assist you. I'm an expert when it comes to food."

Tasha looked at Nula. She was a big woman with a big heart.

Then Tasha smiled, and said, "Thank you, Nula. I'll remember this."

Nula smiled back. "Please do that, but this isn't a time for us to talk. This is a time for you to eat. Enjoy your breakfast." And she disappeared into the kitchen to serve the other people as well.

Tasha started to eat and heard the unspoken words of the people around her. She knew that they were looking at her, staring at her, as if asking, "Who is this stranger?"

Tasha didn't look at them. She had to build her strength, and she couldn't care about other people and their opinions of her.

She enjoyed her meal, yet the whispering around her became stronger.

Then she heard Nula's words: "Come on, haven't you seen a girl before? Leave her alone. Let her eat her meal in peace."

And suddenly, everything stopped. The diners reacted to Nula's words immediately, leaving Tasha alone.

Nula is indeed an expert, Tasha said to herself.

Tasha finished her meal, sat comfortably in her chair, and looked at the people in the restaurant.

Then she saw someone waving at her through the window. A man was waving, inviting her to follow him. That was strange. But Tasha decided to leave her impression aside. She thanked Nula and walked out into the street.

The man hadn't waited for her. She could see him at a distance, and she started to walk toward him. He didn't look at her; he just walked on. But she knew she must follow him.

Suddenly, she lost him. He walked too fast. She stood still and didn't know which way to go. When she turned around to go back, there he was. He was very close to her, yet she hadn't heard him approaching. He was tall and his body was agile, yet peaceful.

"You mustn't leave traces behind you," he said.

"What do you mean?" she asked.

"Each of your footsteps is haunted by your past."

Tasha didn't understand. "Who are you?" she asked.

"My name is Lee," he told her. "If you want to be a free spirit, then first be transparent. Stop leaving traces behind you."

Tasha didn't want to be surprised anymore. She must accept that people knew her, even though she didn't know them. Therefore, all she said was, "Will you teach me how to be transparent?"

"I'm willing to teach you that, so you can face your prison."

Tasha looked at him, as if asking how he knew that.

"I've heard your call," Lee said. "I don't live in town, but I live very close by. Meet me at my house tomorrow morning."

He showed her the way to his house, and within moments, he disappeared.

22. STEP ONE:
BE TRANSPARENT

The "Center-Corner Existence" Technique

As she approached Lee's house the next morning, Tasha saw that it was made of glass. But the closer she got, she realized that there was an invisible wall she couldn't walk through. Yet she remembered that all was possible. If she wanted to enter the house, she would. She was not willing to give up.

So she said out loud her wish to cross the invisible wall. Suddenly, there she was, inside the house, without any effort. But Lee wasn't there.

She sat in front of a small mat on the floor, closed her eyes, and waited.

When she opened her eyes, she saw Lee. "The visible and the invisible are the same," he said. "They are both walls that prevent you from being free. Many people are trying to break the visible walls, as if they are the most important ones. But if one trains his eyes to see the invisible walls, a real change can be made. Do you see the invisible?"

Tasha didn't answer.

And Lee asked again, "Do you see the invisible?"

"I feel the invisible walls, but I don't know if I see the invisible," she answered. "Wherever I go, I hear the same words, the same phrases. I know that no one is cursed. Nevertheless, I sense the prison and its walls all around me, although I can't see it."

"Look below you," Lee instructed.

Suddenly, Tasha felt that the floor beneath her had vanished and she was sitting on air. For a moment, it wasn't a pleasant feeling. But Tasha understood what Lee had tried to tell her.

Then the floor returned, a solid floor.

"Look at me Tasha, and tell me what you see."

And Tasha, without thinking, said, "I see Ceyon."

Lee said, "Look again. What do you see?"

And Tasha replied, "I see the lady who came to my place. I see the man at the gates of Belle. I see Sid, the boy in the hotel. I see Elijah. I see the man in the restaurant, and I see the prison. It's all around me."

"Please, Tasha, look at me and tell me what you see."

And she said, "I don't know if I can see."

Then Lee said, "Thank you. You may stay for a while and rest. Come tomorrow at the same time."

Then he vanished. He simply vanished.

The next morning, Tasha's way to Lee's house was without obstacles, without any invisible walls. She entered the house, saw the mat, but didn't see Lee.

She sat in front of the mat with eyes closed and waited for him. When she opened her eyes, he wasn't there.

She didn't want to call out his name. She felt that this place was too sacred for that. So she continued to sit and wait for him. But Lee didn't arrive.

The thought to leave and come back the next day crossed her mind, but it seemed to her a waste of time, and she couldn't afford this waste. She wanted to live. She wanted to love.

So she said out loud, "Lee, please come."

And he appeared. He didn't sit down; he just stood there.

"I must build my strength. I must face my past and be free, and I don't have any time to spare," she said.

"So, let's begin," Lee said. "In order to be free, you must first know how to be invisible, transparent. To be able to do that, you need to learn the 'Center-Corner Existence' technique. This means being in the center and in the corner at the same time."

"Being at the center," he continued, "attracts people's full attention to you, while at the corner, people don't see you, as if you are invisible. The skill is learning to be at the center without drawing attention."

"Why is it so important?" Tasha asked.

"It will give you the freedom to be present, without being noticed, without leaving any traces," Lee answered. "It is the mastery of diversion, which allows you to control the amount of attention you wish to draw, by mastering the degree of your presence.

"I'll teach you how to shift your presence so that you can move, according to your wish, from being fully present to being fully transparent, yet still remain at the center."

And then he added, "You will be able to remain fully transparent only for a while, so use it wisely."

Lee showed Tasha how she could shift herself from being fully present to being completely transparent and safe at the same time. He trained her to take it to a form of art.

"Now take it into your life and practice it," he told her. "And when you sense that it's yours, come back here. You don't have to tell me in advance, just come."

Tasha thanked him and went out, back to the town.

It was already night. She went straight to the restaurant. She wanted to meet the man she had seen on the night of her arrival, the one who looked like the man at the gates. She must find out who he was.

It was dinnertime. And he was there, sitting alone. She knew that he saw her when she came in, but he made no gesture to let her know. She could ask Nula who he was, but she didn't want to attract attention. She wanted to learn how to be transparent, without leaving traces.

She sat down at the table next to his. Nula was happy to give her some food. The man didn't look at her.

She turned to him and said, "Hello, how are you?"

"Oh, it's you," he said. "I'm fine, and you? How are you getting along in town?"

"I'm fine, too," she replied. "Do you live here?"

The man didn't reply. He went back to his meal as if he were a stranger again. Tasha wanted to ask more, but she remembered Lee's words and decided to use the Center-Corner Existence technique.

So she asked, "Are there any interesting places to visit in this town?"

The man laughed. "One can tell you are a stranger. This town is quite dull. There aren't many interesting sights to visit here."

"My name is Tasha," she said, and offered her hand. But he didn't offer his in return and didn't say his name.

All he said was, "It's different, your name. Very unique, like you."

Tasha knew that she was not using the Center-Corner Existence technique in the right way. He still thought of her as unique, and she wanted to be plain for just one moment. Her name was unique, her look was unique, her life was unique.

For just one moment, can't I be ordinary? she thought.

She left the restaurant. She knew that she would meet this man again, but she must come ready.

Over the next few days, wherever she went, she tried to divide the attention she attracted in order to be transparent.

One day she came to visit Nula at her house. The children were there, and they were happy to see her. Tasha had become a good friend of this family. They loved her. They never asked questions. They just enjoyed her for who she was, and they respected her privacy.

When she came in, the kids didn't run to her as they usually did. They just passed by her saying, "Hello, Tasha," and "Hi, Tasha," and that was all. For a moment, she was an ordinary girl who had come to visit her friends. Tasha smiled. *The Technique is working,* she said to herself.

Now that she had applied the Center-Corner Existence technique with the children, Tasha knew that she had to go and see Lee again, facing her next step. However, she first wanted to meet the man again in the restaurant, and she didn't want to wait. So she decided to go there the next evening, and only then would she visit Lee.

23. IAN

As Deep as the Ocean

The evening came, and Tasha entered the restaurant. She didn't see the man. She sat at the same table as the other day. Nula, as always, was happy to see her. To Tasha, Nula was like a peaceful island, the only person who seemed constant. And Tasha appreciated it.

After a while, the man entered the restaurant. Tasha behaved as if she hadn't noticed him and continued to eat her soup. She sensed that he hesitated about whether to sit at the same table where he had been usually sitting. Despite his hesitation, he walked to the table and sat down. He didn't say a word.

After finishing her soup, she looked up at him and said, "Hello."

"Hello," he replied and continued eating.

Tasha didn't say anything more. Yet she wanted to know more about this man. She felt that he was a key for her, a key to an invisible door.

Eventually, Nula came toward them, and with her natural warmth said, "Tasha, please meet Ian. Ian, this is Tasha. If people sit next to each other more than once," she continued, "they should at least know each other's names. And now it is up to you if you want to talk." Then she disappeared into the big restaurant.

In her heart, Tasha thanked Nula. She couldn't have asked for better help. Then she turned to Ian and said, "Hello, Ian."

"Hello," he answered.

"Nula said it's up to us whether we want to talk or not," she said. "What do you say?"

Since she sat to his side rather than in front of him, Ian couldn't see Tasha fully. In order to speak with her, he must turn his entire body. And she knew that without his turning, a conversation couldn't happen.

Ian turned and looked at her. He gazed into her eyes with a sharp look. But Tasha wasn't offended at all. She was calm and peaceful, and he couldn't take his eyes off her.

Tasha knew that as long as he hadn't looked into her eyes, he could have stayed remote and aloof. But now that he had looked, a connection had been made and a conversation started, although it was unspoken. There were no words at all.

In his eyes, Tasha saw pain and heard a cry. It wasn't a cry for help. It was only a cry. His eyes were as deep as the ocean. She felt as if she were swimming in this big ocean, and it was endless.

Suddenly, a loud noise came from one of the other tables. People were arguing. The ocean disappeared. She saw a veil covering Ian's eyes. Ian had become a stranger again. Without saying a word, he returned to his meal, as if nothing had happened. She felt a kind of ache, and she didn't understand why.

She didn't want to say more to Ian. She felt that it wasn't important anymore. She knew that Ian was a key for her. But somehow, the door had changed. It was not the door she had thought it to be. For one moment, she felt a strong yearning to reach the ocean. She had almost forgotten the ocean. And there was Ian.

24. THIRD WAY

A Date from God

That night Tasha couldn't sleep. The sight of Ian's eyes—the
deep blue ocean, without fences or walls—wouldn't let her go. The
ocean was like fresh water poured on the dry earth of the desert.

Tasha knew she must meet Ceyon on her way to the ocean.
But all that she wanted to do was to see the vast ocean in Ian's
eyes. Her feelings tempted her to follow the ocean right now, as
if saying to her, *Leave Ceyon alone, you don't need to face him. Go to
the ocean. Go now.*

She had become transparent for that long moment in the
restaurant, but it hadn't made her happy. She thought that by
being transparent she would be safe. Therefore, she had let the
ocean in without any guard, without any second thoughts. And
she felt pain.

The next morning, she was on her way to Lee's house, ready for
the second step. She didn't want her feelings to weaken her. She
must remain clear. She must remain sharp.

It was a sunny day, and Tasha enjoyed the walk and the fresh
air. On her way, she noticed a coin on the ground. She bent to
pick up the coin, and when she stood again, Ian was there. For a

moment, she was speechless. She had never seen him in daylight. He was much younger than she had thought.

So much pain and so young, she said to herself.

Ian asked, "Where are you going?"

"It's a nice day, and I'm enjoying the walk and feeling the sun."

"Let's walk together," he said.

Tasha again faced the struggle. She wanted to go with Ian, but knew that she needed to visit Lee. If Ian was the ocean, then Lee was Ceyon. She couldn't reach the ocean before facing Ceyon.

"Come on, let's walk," Ian insisted.

And Tasha said, "All right, but only for a little while."

Ian looked at her and asked, "Do you have to go somewhere?"

But all Tasha said was, "Let's go."

Tasha didn't know the town well. She knew only two roads: the road that took her to Lee's house, and the one that took her to the restaurant. She didn't want to know more than those two ways. But Ian took her a third way, and she followed him.

Ian knew the town very well. He showed her the narrow streets, which led to nice houses. He showed her the lively shops, which sold fresh fruits and vegetables and all kinds of other goods.

He didn't talk much. He didn't talk about himself at all. For Tasha, this was fine. She wasn't interested in hearing more about him at that moment. She was just there. Yet when she looked at him, she could still see the veil in his eyes. The ocean was not accessible to her.

They reached a small café surrounded by trees and flowers. Everything in the café was made of wood, and the atmosphere was welcoming. Ian invited Tasha to sit and have something to drink. But Tasha sensed she should go to Lee's house. Her feelings wanted her to accept Ian's invitation, but her senses were sending her to Lee. Ian saw for a moment the struggle in Tasha. He asked her whether everything was all right.

"Ian, I would love to sit with you," she said, "but I must go now. Let's do it another time."

Ian didn't ask where she was going, yet Tasha discerned a kind of pain in his eyes. Still, she knew that she couldn't stay. She had to go, but she couldn't explain to him why.

Ian walked with her to the place where they had met. All he said was, "Good-bye, Tasha. Have a good day." And he walked away.

Tasha felt the pain again, the same pain she had felt the night before. Nevertheless, she was determined to meet with Lee in order to face Ceyon.

On her way to Lee's house, she remembered the coin she had found. When she looked at it, she saw a palm tree and the writing: "A DATE FROM GOD." She felt a yearning to follow the third way Ian offered her. But for the time being, she must forget this way. She must understand all those faces that had come to visit her—the lady in the lace, the man at the gate, Elijah, Sid. She must confront her past.

The ocean was there, and Ian was there, too. But Tasha was here, and the faces were here. There was no connection. It was as if they were in different dimensions, as if there was no connection at all.

25. STEP TWO: BE VACANT

No Opinions, No Reactions

Lee was waiting for her at the gates of his house.

Tasha walked toward him and said, "Hello, Lee. I am here for the next step."

Lee said, "Tasha, why didn't you come when you were ready? Why do you come only now?"

"I have no explanation to give you," she replied. "All I can say is that I am ready now."

Lee was quiet for a moment and then said, "Very well. Let's move on to the second step. Follow me, and don't ask any questions. It's not the right time for them."

Tasha followed Lee along a narrow path until he stopped and said, "Look down and tell me what you see."

She looked down and saw a deep abyss. She realized that they were on the edge of a cliff.

Lee asked her, "What do you see, Tasha?"

"I see Ceyon."

And Lee asked her again, "What do you see, Tasha?"

"I see Ian," she replied.

And Lee kept on asking, "What do you see?"

"The depth of my soul, and I don't like it."

"I didn't ask whether you like it or not. All I asked is: What do you see? Don't deviate from the question, Tasha. What do you see?"

"Great despair." Then she said, "I don't see anything anymore."

Lee asked her to sit down and listen very carefully. They sat on the edge of the cliff. It was dangerous, but Lee didn't seem concerned. Tasha wasn't afraid. She was not afraid to die.

Lee saw that, and said to her, "Tasha, you didn't see the fear of death, because you don't know it. But you saw your prison and didn't like it.

"The second step is to be vacant. It is not enough to be transparent. When you are transparent, people won't notice you, but it doesn't mean that you can see them. In order to see people, to really see them, you must be vacant. This means to be with no opinions and no reactions, no jury and no accused. If you have even one opinion about what you observe, you will not be able to see. The elusive perception of existence is caused by the judgments that people exercise in their daily lives. Their opinions turn them blind."

Then he asked, "Look at me, Tasha. Am I young?"

"You look young."

"And now? Do I look young?"

"Now you look older than before," she replied.

"So, am I young, or am I old?"

And Tasha answered, "I don't know."

"Tasha, I didn't do anything to appear older. My question gave you the false impression that I had done something, but I hadn't done anything. It was in your mind, rather than in the outside existence."

Tasha admitted to herself that he had really appeared older to her. Then she understood the trap.

So she said, "I want to see. I want to see what is real. I don't care about all the other things."

Lee said, "I'm willing to show you how to open your eyes and see what is real. But I must warn you: Sometimes it hurts. Our mind constantly compensates for the things we don't want to see.

It creates endless stories to mask what exists, to help our emotions endure life. Do you want to see, even though it will hurt sometimes? Your heart must face unpleasant experiences in order to face what is real. Do you consent? Without your consent, I can't show you anything."

"I want to see," she said, without any hesitation. "And I'm willing to pay the price."

"Here is the assignment I want to give you. I want you to go back to your life and interact with people. Go talk to them, observe, and see their own stories rather than yours.

"In order to see things as they are, you must cover your eyes with a veil. When we look into the depths of another's eyes, we usually see a reflection of ourselves. And you don't want to meet yourself in the eyes of others. You want to see the people and their stories.

"Therefore, you should keep this veil all day long for the next three days. You can't raise the veil for anyone. Listen carefully, Tasha—not for anyone. While you are speaking with people, see who they are and what they are looking for in their lives. Avoid judgment of any kind, and leave your opinions behind. Take three days. If after these three days you still see *your* stories in other people's eyes, take the time you need, and only then come back. Is that clear?"

"Yes, it's clear," she replied.

"Have a pleasant day, Tasha. I must go now," Lee said, and in an instant, he was gone.

26. LENA

That Was All

Tasha entered her room. She lay on the bed and took a deep breath. She needed it. Did she want to see? To really see? Was she willing to pay the price?

When she had stood in front of Lee, she felt it so deeply, but now, it had faded. She wanted to be with Ian, she wanted to talk with him. She wanted to rest rather than face the people in the town. Suddenly, she noticed she didn't call the town by its name. To her it was just another town, not a place to live. If she called the town by its name, she would have to call the people by their names. Beside the few people that she knew, she wanted to stay a stranger. She didn't belong to this town, and she didn't want to change her relationship to it. She was a stranger who must deal with her depths in order to be free. That was all. The town was not important. But Ian, what about Ian?

She remembered the depth of his eyes, the ocean, the freedom that she saw. And she asked herself if it was her story she saw or Ian's story.

She needed rest, but only a momentary rest. She knew that she couldn't turn away from her decision to face Ceyon first and be free.

When Tasha woke up, it was dark outside. She went to the restaurant and met Nula. Nula hugged Tasha and told her that her meal was on its way. All she had to do was have a seat. That was all. Nula was like that. Everything was so easy and natural. Tasha wished that her life would be the same. Everything would be simple, and that would be all.

Ian wasn't there. She sat at the same table as the evenings before. She couldn't decide if she wanted Ian to come or not. She had an assignment to fulfill. Although her heart longed to follow Ian, she wanted to be vacant, to be a void, to see. Otherwise, the prison would keep surrounding her, wherever she might go.

Then, Tasha saw a woman sitting two tables from her. She saw the sorrow in her eyes, and she decided to talk to her. She went to the woman and told her that her name was Tasha, and that she thought it would be nice to join her and eat together.

The woman looked up at her and said, "If it pleases you, you can sit here. But I won't be a good companion today."

Tasha sat down at the woman's table and asked Nula to bring her meal there. Tasha didn't say anything, and the woman didn't say anything, either. She ate, and her eyes didn't leave the food.

Tasha didn't mind that the woman wasn't friendly. She said, "I don't know whether you know it or not, but you seem like a lovely lady, and that's why I wanted to sit next to you."

The woman looked at her with surprise, as if she didn't believe Tasha's words. Then she said to her, "You don't have to comfort me. I'm fine. I'm not miserable."

"I'm not comforting you. I wouldn't have offered to sit next to you if I hadn't wanted to speak to you. Perhaps you are having one of those days, but that happens to all of us."

The woman looked at her and asked, "You're new in town, aren't you?"

"Yes, I am."

"How long are you going to stay?" The woman asked.

"I don't really know."

"What are you doing in our small town? Look at you. You are a beautiful girl—the world could be yours."

"I find your town very nice," said Tasha, "and I've decided to stay for a while."

Then the woman said, "My name is Lena, and I'm happy to meet you, Tasha. Welcome to our town. But now I must be alone. Please don't think I'm unkind. I just need some time to figure out my life again, and I need to do it alone. Thank you for coming to sit with me; it was very kind. I'm sure we will meet again."

Tasha left the table and went back to her own table. She had seen great despair in Lena's eyes, but she didn't know whether it was her own sorrow or Lena's. All she knew was that Lena didn't suffer from self-pity. She was strong enough to face her life by herself. And Tasha liked it. Yet she remembered Lee's words—that her opinions were an obstacle if she wanted to see, to really see what was real.

And then Ian came in. Tasha was happy to see him. She was surprised that he sat at his table rather than joining her. But again she saw that this was only her opinion, and she wanted to see what was real.

"Hi, Tasha," said Ian. "How was your day?"

"Fine, and yours?"

"Fine. Just fine," he replied.

The music in Ian's words was as if he was trying to tell her something without saying it. Tasha waited to see what more he would say, but he didn't look at her. He had become a total stranger again, as if the morning they spent together had never happened.

Ian didn't speak throughout the whole meal, and Tasha didn't disturb his silence. She wanted to talk to him. She wanted to know more about him, but it wasn't the right time. She understood that Ian had his own past, which seemed to haunt him, and he would have to face his own *that day* in order to reach the ocean.

She saw all of that clearly. For a moment, she wanted it to be different, yet she knew that her opinions and expectations were merely an obstacle. She must face reality as it was, rather than how she wanted it to be. Ian was real. He had a long way to go—the same as she did. And they could not walk that path together.

27. A MIRACLE

The Last Day of Summer

Morning had come. Tasha sensed the chill. Summer was preparing to leave a place vacant for autumn. Tasha felt that like the summer, she must leave a vacant place in herself and welcome whatever would come—whether it was autumn, winter, or strong storms. Deep in her heart, she knew that she wanted to fill the empty space with the spring to come. She wanted the trees to blossom, to see buds growing into beautiful flowers. She wanted the sun to be soft in a clear sky. She longed for spring, yet sensed the chill. Autumn was on its way.

For the first time, Tasha wasn't one with Nature. Her deep desire wasn't in harmony with her surroundings. A struggle was there. And no matter where she looked, it was simply there.

Tasha decided to go outside into the streets. She wanted to visit the places she had been with Ian the day before. She wanted to relive what they saw. She looked at the coin that said, "A DATE FROM GOD," and she started to think about the strange coincidence.

But then a decisive voice within her told her that she was drifting toward superstition: *The illusions of the heart are the most dangerous. They are strong and seem so real.*

Tasha answered the voice, "But they *are* real."

The voice kept speaking. *The illusions of the heart are the most dangerous. They cover reality with soft blankets. They tell you fantastic stories about romantic kingdoms, but they are all false.*

And the voice continued: *Never go to places you have already been. Create your present.*

The voice had given her a gift, but it also had given her a thorn.

Tasha walked down the street, letting her feet take her to meet people. She must see in their eyes whether the stories were her stories or theirs. She wanted to see what was real, yet her feelings were taking her in a different direction, yearning for a simple existence. She felt that those illusions of the heart, those false kingdoms of constant spring, were so attractive, so tempting. She knew that it wasn't real. But she also knew that this was a part of *her* reality.

She didn't want to go to the restaurant, so she just walked down the street. Suddenly, Ian was there. Tasha was happy, but didn't show it. It was her story, and she didn't know if it was Ian's as well.

She looked at him and said, "Hello, Ian. How are you?"

"I'm well," he said. "Where are you going?"

"I don't really know. I felt like walking along the street. These are the last days of summer, and I wanted to enjoy them."

"Then come with me," Ian said.

Tasha followed him and was surprised that he took her the same way she always took to Lee's house.

Suddenly, she thought that Ian might know Lee, and she liked this idea.

But to her surprise, when they reached where Lee's house should have been, the house wasn't there. It was a green place, although it was the end of summer. A small creek was there. You could hear the water flowing slowly, as if taking its time.

"You wanted to see a nice place in this town," Ian said. "Well, this is the nicest one. No one knows how to explain it, but this place is always green, and the water flows constantly in the creek. It's a kind of miracle."

Tasha didn't know what to say. She had visited the place the day before, and Lee's house had stood there. Now there was no house and no Lee.

They sat on the bank of the creek. Tasha put her legs in the water and liked it. She invited Ian to do the same. But he didn't do so. He just sat next to her.

Then Tasha asked, "How do you explain this miracle, Ian?"

"Do we have to explain miracles?"

"We had better not." Tasha laughed.

"Look at the water, Tasha."

Tasha looked at the water. It was clean and clear.

"The water makes a reflection," Ian said. "When you look in it, you can see yourself. Try it."

"I've never seen my reflection before," Tasha said to him.

Ian looked at her and couldn't hide his surprise. "You haven't ever seen yourself, your reflection?"

"No, I haven't."

Then he said, "Look into my eyes, Tasha. Can you see yourself?"

Tasha looked into his eyes and saw some fear. Then she saw the big blue ocean again. It was endless. She didn't feel anything except a wonderful feeling of coming home. Tasha didn't know how long she was looking into Ian's eyes. It was as if there were no time or space.

Suddenly, she sensed great fear. She had forgotten to veil her eyes and remembered Lee's instructions: "You can't raise this veil for anyone. Not for anyone."

Then she heard Ian's words: "Tasha, what's going on?"

Tasha was quiet for a moment, and then she said, "I can't explain, Ian, but I must go."

"Where are you going? What happened? Tasha, you can't run away all the time."

Tasha remembered Ceyon's words about sneaking off at night, about facing people. But still, she didn't know what to say. She felt that Ian was taking her beyond space and time. She felt safe next to him, as if she could be lost in his ocean and still be safe. But Lee had shown her the way to Ceyon. Ian's way and Lee's way were not the same. How could she explain these things to Ian?

So she said to him, "You must trust me. There are many things happening in my life right now, and it's just too complicated to explain. I must go, Ian. I simply must."

Tasha left the place. She knew that this was the last day of summer. She couldn't ask Nature for even one more day. Autumn had come, and the storm had come as well.

28. THE WATER

The One Who Doesn't See the Shadows

Tasha didn't want to see anyone. She just wanted to sit down and figure out her life.

She was near the hotel when she saw Nula. Nula, with her big smile and big hug, understood that Tasha wasn't at her best. But Nula never asked questions. She offered the comfort of food. She knew how to nurture people, and Tasha was one of them.

Tasha found herself in Nula's restaurant, in front of a bowl of soup made especially for her. She was trying to decipher what had happened when she heard someone say, "I think it would be nice to join you and eat together."

She looked up and saw Lena standing before her, so Tasha said, "Please, have a seat."

Lena sat down. "Perhaps you're having one of those days. That happens to all of us."

Tasha laughed. *Dear Lena,* she thought, *you said the right words.*

Tasha looked into Lena's eyes and didn't see the despair that she had seen the day before. Had the despair been Lena's, or hers? Regardless, it wasn't there anymore.

"I see you're feeling better," Tasha said.

"You see well," Lena replied. "I'm better today. But I don't think that I'm past those days. Are you, Tasha?"

"No, I am not."

"I just wanted to say hello and thank you for last night," Lena said. "You were kind and I appreciate it, but I don't have to sit with you if you need time for yourself."

"Thank you, Lena. I think I do need some time for myself."

Then Lena got up and said, "You're a lovely lady, Tasha. Although it's funny to call you a *lady*." Lena laughed, and went on her way.

Tasha ate her soup not knowing what to do. Should she go to Lee and tell him what had happened, although he probably knew about it by now, or follow her assignment as if it were a new day, a new beginning? She knew she had to face Ceyon. Yet whenever she saw Ian, he captured her whole being. When Ian wasn't present, she knew that Ceyon was her next step.

Lee probably knows by now, Tasha thought. *So if he wants to say something to me, he will find a way.* She must go on. A long way remained ahead of her, and she must not see Ian for the time being. She knew that. And it was real.

When she left the restaurant on the way to her room, Ian was there. He was waiting for her. Tasha knew that she must face him, talk to him. He wasn't an obstacle. He was a person, and maybe, a friend.

She went straight to him and said, "Hi, Ian."

And he said, "Tasha, you must explain what's going on. One moment you're full of life, you are so present, and the next moment you're full of doubts and distant thoughts. What's going on? Please stop running away."

Tasha felt that she couldn't tell Ian parts of her story. She wasn't ready for that yet, but she couldn't run away either.

"Ian, I came to this town because I needed to figure out my life. On our journeys, we walk alone. I may make some friends, but I still walk alone. I don't know when the time to talk about my journey will come. All I know is that I have to follow my way. Please trust me, Ian. I must do it alone. Each of us must deal with life alone."

Tasha stopped talking, and Ian looked into her eyes and said, "One moment you're full of laughter, you're smiling . . . you're like the sun. And the next moment, you're distant and remote. Who are you, Tasha?"

"That's a good question, Ian," Tasha answered quietly, "but it's for me to decipher, only for me." She said good-bye and walked away.

She felt the beating of her heart. She didn't want to go. She wanted to stay. But she hadn't come to this town to meet Ian. She had come to meet herself, through Ceyon. She didn't really know who she was, but she knew that it was for her to find out.

She went to her room, but she couldn't find a place for herself. She was restless. She remembered Ceyon's words: "Welcome to my kingdom." She remembered the lady who said, "If you don't remember me, I can't tell you another word." All these words, all these faces danced around her, surrounded her, as if the outside wouldn't leave her space to live in.

Suddenly, she got up and went outside the hotel. She walked to the creek where she had sat with Ian. She must look into *her own* eyes this time. If the water was as clear as it had been in the morning, she would look into it, into her eyes, and she would see her own depths, her stories, her secrets.

The creek was there. Nothing had changed. The water was as clear as ever. She had never looked into her own eyes. She had never seen her own reflection. She remembered the spirit of Lia's words: "I don't care about the consequences or misusing the power. First live, and then deal with the consequences. You don't have any other choice. You simply don't."

Tasha bent toward the water. She gazed deeply into it to find her depths, her stories. But, to her surprise, her body wasn't reflected in the water. She saw the reflection of trees and clouds in the water, but she couldn't see herself. The water was clear, but her eyes weren't there. Tasha sat down quietly.

Am I a part of someone else's story? she asked herself.

Suddenly, she heard a voice from the outside saying, "Yes, you are."

"Are the people I've met a part of my story?"

And the voice said, "Yes, they are."

"So, who is real? Who is the one whose story we are all parts of?"

"All of you," the voice replied.

Then Tasha asked, "Why am I not a part of the river's story? I looked into it and couldn't see myself."

And the voice said, "Because you don't see the shadows of existence."

Tasha was silent. At that moment all words stopped. All thoughts vanished. All emotions faded away. There was only an endless silence, an empty space, a void. The one who doesn't see the shadows, at that very moment, was fully present.

29. STEP THREE:
SEEING THE SHADOWS

To See What Was Always There

Tasha opened her eyes and Lee was there. It seemed as if time and space didn't touch her, as if she had come from a different dimension.

Tasha didn't say anything. She needed some time to get back to reality. Lee didn't say a word, either. He waited for her. Kindly, he was waiting for her.

After a while, Lee said, "Come Tasha, we must go now. The next step is waiting for you."

Tasha followed him, and although it was at the same place of the creek, they found themselves, in an unexplained way, in Lee's house. It was as if they had entered another dimension.

Tasha sat down, and Lee sat calmly in front of her. There was a silence they both respected.

Then Tasha said, "You are going to teach me about shadows, those dark shadows that interfere with my life."

"That's right," Lee replied. "Not seeing the shadows of existence, of people, is your shadow. Beware of attributing to people qualities they don't possess. This naïvety is not about being pure and honest; it's about being stupid and blind. You must see people as they are, rather than as you want them to be. Don't stop seeing their beauty. But without seeing their shadows, you cannot see. You cannot see their full existence. Are you ready to see the shadows of life, of people, of existence?

"Yes, I am," Tasha answered.

So Lee said, "Welcome to the kingdom of darkness. Welcome to the kingdom of twisted perception. Welcome to the kingdom of temptation, jealousy, greed, and loneliness. Welcome to the kingdom of fear. Welcome to the kingdom."

Tasha shivered. She knew that she couldn't avoid entering this kingdom. She knew she couldn't avoid the dark side of life if she wanted to meet Ceyon, if she wanted to meet herself.

"I'm ready. I'm ready to see the shadows."

"Look at me, Tasha. What do you see when you look at this orange?" Suddenly an orange was in his hand.

"I see an orange."

"Look at the orange now. What do you see?"

And Tasha said with a burst of laughter, "I see some potatoes."

"Now, look again," Lee said. "What do you see now?"

"I see Ceyon."

"Look into his eyes, Tasha. What do you see?"

And Tasha replied, "I see the orange in them."

"And what does it mean?" Lee asked

"That the orange was too orange. I mean, that I was too . . ." And suddenly she stopped.

Lee didn't say another word. He let her see what was always there, and it wasn't easy for her.

Deep inside she felt an ache, and she said, "I couldn't believe it then, and I can't believe it now. Ceyon has a shadow."

"It's not a matter of belief," Lee said. "It's whether you see the shadow or not. It's a matter of clear sight. What do you see, Tasha?"

"I see a trace of his shadow. I see his jealousy, and I can't erase it. It's simply there. No matter what I do, it is there."

"It was always there, but you weren't able to see it. It's as simple as that. Do you want to see the shadows, Tasha? Are you willing to pay the price? Are you willing to feel the ache?"

"Yes, I am."

"If you really want to see," Lee continued, "this is what you have to do. Go back to the town. Meet the people and see their shadows. In order to see the shadow, you can't look straight at the person. You should look at his or her side. The shadow is always at one's side. Look at it with an open heart. Don't try to eliminate the ache. Your heart should be able to face reality as it is, not as you expect it to be. When you feel that you can see the shadows of people, come back to me. You will know when. I'll be here."

Tasha stayed at Lee's house for a while. She needed some rest. She knew she was going to enter the kingdom. She knew she was going to meet the shadows of people, the shadows of life, the shadows of existence. She knew that her life wouldn't be the same anymore. The dark side of life was waiting for her. And she was ready for it.

30. A PAINFUL SECRET

Daring to Live

It was already dark when Tasha left Lee's house. The night welcomed her. She went to the restaurant to see Nula. She wanted to see the big lady with her big smile and big hug.

What is her shadow? Tasha asked herself.

When she entered the restaurant, Ian was there. But Tasha wanted to see Nula rather than Ian. So she went to Ian and said, "Hello," yet she didn't join him.

Ian looked at her but remained silent.

Tasha sat at her own table and waited for Nula. Then she saw her. Nula came from the kitchen and was happy to see Tasha.

"How are you, Tasha?" Nula asked.

"I'm fine," Tasha answered. "I see that you're very busy today."

"Yes, I'm busy, but I love it. Look at all the people in the restaurant. They come in, very tense from their hard work, and they usually leave the restaurant with a big smile. This is my small contribution to people. And I love it."

Tasha loved Nula. It was as if she had been born with a heart big enough to nurture the whole community by herself. Then Tasha looked at Nula's side. She hesitated, not sure she wanted to see Nula's shadow. But she looked, nevertheless, and suddenly saw the pain in her. She saw that Nula had a painful secret that she kept to herself. Gradually Tasha saw the whole picture: Nula couldn't have children. She wanted to have many children, but none of her children was her own. Nula felt cursed. Therefore, she had overworked herself by nurturing the whole community.

For a moment, Tasha wanted to hug her and rescue her from her suffering and pain. But she knew that everyone has his or her own journey, and she couldn't save Nula from the pain in hers.

Nula waved her hands in front of Tasha's face, as if wanting to wake her up. "What do you want to eat?"

Tasha said, "I would like to have your wonderful soup."

"One soup is on its way. And you, Ian, what can I serve you?"

"I'll have your wonderful soup as well," Ian said.

"So shall it be," said Nula, and went back to the kitchen. For a big lady, she was light in her movements.

Tasha thought about Nula's story. It had always been there to see, yet she hadn't seen it. For a moment, she felt so blind, so stupid. But she knew that she shouldn't think about that. She wanted to see, and she took upon herself to see the shadows, to really see them, and that was all that was important at that very moment.

"Hey Tasha, where are you?" asked Ian.

Tasha turned and said, "I am here and there. How are you, Ian?"

"I'm fine," he said. And then he added, "You look different. You are not the same as you were this morning."

"I'm *not* the same," she said.

"What has happened?"

"I'm simply not the same," she replied.

Tasha wanted to talk with Ian. She wanted to tell him more about herself. She remembered Lee's words about daring to live with an open heart. Yet still she felt that this wasn't the right time to open her heart to Ian.

Tasha glanced quickly at Ian, too quickly to observe his shadow. She wanted to see, yet she didn't. Was she afraid that his shadow would eliminate his beauty? Tasha loved the truth, but she now felt that the truth could steal the images she had in mind. Was the ocean she had seen in Ian's eyes truly his?

She heard Ian say, "Good-bye Tasha," as he left the restaurant. She wanted to say, "Don't go. Don't go yet." But she didn't say anything.

That night in bed, before sleep, she heard the voice within herself saying, *Don't go. Don't go yet.* She felt the struggle.

What a strange world, she thought to herself. *I don't want to choose. I want both truth and love, and I'm not willing to compromise.*

And the voice kept on saying, *Don't go. Don't go yet. I love you.* Tasha felt the ache. She didn't struggle. In fact, she became the struggle.

31. THE EMPTY HOUSE

So Many Colors, So Many Shadows

In the morning, Tasha wanted to go outside to meet people. She wanted to see their shadows.

When she walked out of the hotel, Ian was there. "Come, Tasha. Come with me," he said. "Just follow me."

Tasha felt the struggle again. Still, she followed him.

They walked through the streets of the town until Ian stopped and said, "See this house, Tasha? I was born here. The house is empty now. It has been empty for the last twenty years. This house reminds me of the days with my parents and my brother."

Ian didn't mention before that he had a brother. Tasha immediately thought about the man at the gates, but she didn't say anything.

"I loved my parents. My mother was beautiful and full of life. We didn't see much of my father, but when we saw him, he showed us kindness and love. My brother was older than me. He was four when I was born. His name was Luke. We lived in this house for six happy years. Then, one sunny day, when I woke up, I found myself alone in an empty house. And since then, the house has been empty."

Tasha sensed the pain in Ian's voice. "Do you come here often?" she asked.

"No, I don't," he replied. "To me this is the graveyard of my family. It's as if this empty house is cursed. No one wants to live here. They are afraid that it will touch them, that the tragedy will strike them as well."

"Do you miss them?"

"Sometimes. But after twenty years, I don't remember their faces anymore."

Tasha was quiet. She stood next to Ian. She could hear his heart beating. She wanted to hug him, but she stayed still.

Then Ian asked, "Are you an empty house as well, Tasha?"

Tasha was surprised. She hadn't expected such a question. She felt that the question was wrapped in pain. Tasha didn't know what to say. She couldn't offer him real friendship. She wanted him to trust her. But she knew that it was a difficult request. How could he trust her, when she wouldn't open her heart to him?

"Are you, Tasha? Are you an empty house?"

"I don't know, Ian. I really don't."

They stood there for a while, silently. The atmosphere was sacred. It was as if they had allowed themselves to reach a different place.

Tasha didn't want to leave. It was a special moment. Yet she knew that hearing Ian's story could not take the place of seeing his shadow. She must see his shadow through her eyes rather than his. But she wasn't ready to see it yet.

Then she said, "Let's go, Ian. We should leave now."

They didn't speak. The sacred silence followed them until they reached the hotel.

"Good-bye, Tasha," Ian said. "Have a good day." And he left.

She didn't want him to go, but deep inside herself she thanked him for doing so.

Tasha didn't want to stay in the hotel, so she walked down the street and found herself heading toward the market. She knew she wouldn't have to talk to people there. All she wanted to do was see their shadows.

The market was full of life. There were many stalls with fruit, vegetables, meat, and dairy foods. So many colors, so many people.

She walked along the paved street and looked at the man who was shouting, trying to sell "the best fresh fruit ever." He was strong enough to shout all day without getting tired. But when Tasha looked at his side, she saw aggression and loneliness. She saw how this man was chasing friendship, and at the end of the day, he was all alone. His pursuit of friendship was aggressive, as if he were desperate, and his kindness was forced. Tasha understood that in a twisted way, he tried to make friends in the market, but his strong, loud voice left him with all his fresh fruit unsold. The people didn't like to buy from him. The merchandise was fresh indeed, but this man didn't understand that life isn't about fresh merchandise. It's always about fresh relationships. It was all there, in front of her, for her to see. When she saw him, she saw the whole picture of him.

Try to be kind, lonely man, she said to herself. *Try to be kind.* But she said this only to herself. It wasn't her journey; it was his. And she respected it.

She walked on and saw a little girl who came to buy some fresh vegetables. The girl was very young. Tasha looked at her side and saw fear and sadness. She saw her story. She saw that her father had left her mother and her. She saw that the mother couldn't be responsible for her own life. This girl had taken the responsibility for her mother. She was so young, so little, yet so old.

Then Tasha saw an old lady walking along the street, looking as if she hadn't come to buy anything. When Tasha looked at her side, she saw bitterness and jealousy. She saw that the lady's story was about making other people's lives miserable. She wouldn't let go of people, and, therefore, people left her alone. All she had was her daily march down this *via dolorosa* of life.

So many colors. So many people. So many shadows.

32. LUKE

A Matter of the Heart

The day passed. Tasha knew that the time had come for her to see Ian's shadow. She couldn't avoid it any longer. She didn't know if she was ready to face what was there, but she couldn't wait. She wanted to see Ian, and there he was, right in front of the hotel, as if he was waiting for her.

"Let's go, Ian. Let's go," she said.

Ian followed her. She didn't know where she was going; she simply let her feet lead the way. She wanted open fields. She didn't want streets or houses or people.

When they reached an old tree, Tasha sat down and so did Ian. To see Ian's shadow was not a matter of an assignment. It was a matter of the heart.

Then she asked, "Have you ever thought about leaving this town?"

"Yes, I have. I've even left, but I came back. The empty house haunted me, and I knew that I wouldn't have a future if I didn't deal with the past. So I came back, I returned to the empty house. As a matter of fact, I returned only a few days before you arrived."

Tasha looked at him and asked, "Do you know a town by the name of Belle?"

"No, I don't," he replied.

Tasha felt that she needed to leave the story of the man at the gates aside for the time being. So she asked, "Did you ever hear anything from your family? Did they ever try to reach you?"

"No. Since *that day,* I've never heard from them or about them."

"Did you try to look for them?"

Ian was quiet for a moment and then said, "Twenty years is a long time, Tasha."

"Is it?"

Ian didn't answer. He sat quietly. But Tasha could sense the storm within him. She could also sense the storm within herself. She looked at Ian's side and waited. She knew that she was going to see the whole story of Ian, not merely fragments of it.

Suddenly, Tasha saw Ian's brother, Luke. He looked like Ian. He had the same features, but his journey was different. The Shohonks asked for him, and his parents couldn't bear to give him away. Tasha saw how his parents had received threats because they wouldn't give Luke up. In spite of the harshness of the threats, they protected both Ian and Luke from the truth, and as the threats strengthened, the parents decided to do whatever was in their power to protect Luke from this destiny.

One day, they disappeared with Luke to hide him from the Shohonk people. They left Ian behind, for they felt he would be safer not being on the run with them. They didn't warn him or tell him that they were leaving, because they didn't want the Shohonks to pressure him. But they were naïve to think that they wouldn't be found. Although it took awhile, the Shohonks finally traced them. They burst into their hideaway and ruthlessly, without a drop of kindness, took the boy with them.

Luke and Ian's parents were overwhelmed by grief and guilt. They lost trust in people, in life, and in themselves as parents. In their fragile, traumatized state of being, they thought that Ian would be better without them, and they didn't come back for him.

And what about Luke? Tasha asked herself. But she couldn't see more. It was as if Luke's life didn't belong to Ian's shadow. She saw how Ian had become a lonely wolf and that he had lost trust in people. She looked at Ian's shadow and saw how he had become withdrawn and remote, as if this was the only way to face life. He was trapped in this empty house, and his life was empty as well.

Then she heard Ian say, "Tasha, where did you go?"

But Tasha, who was lost for a moment in Ian's story, just looked at him, as if to say, "I'm here and there."

She felt relief after seeing Ian's shadow. She saw how vulnerable and tender Ian was, yet she knew that she must not underestimate his shadow. Being aloof could be a real hurdle to friendship.

They sat there for a while and didn't talk much. Each of them had had his own *that day.* Since hers, Tasha had been haunted by Ceyon's spirit. Ian was haunted by an empty house. His parents were haunted by the disappearance of Luke. *Each of us,* Tasha thought, *has our own spirits that haunt us, and we must stop running away.*

"Who raised you . . . after *that day?*" Tasha then asked.

"Mother Nature and her good angels," replied Ian.

"What about people? Didn't they help raise you?"

"What about them?" he said.

"You've lost faith in people, haven't you?" Tasha asked.

But Ian didn't answer.

33. STEP FOUR: TRANSCENDING WHAT IS POSSIBLE

Creating a Bridge

When Tasha went to bed that night, she felt she was ready to see Ceyon's shadow in its entirety. It was dark outside. The kingdom of darkness was there for her to enter.

She invited the image of Ceyon to come. She wanted to see him. She wanted to look at his side, but Ceyon's image didn't appear. She couldn't *see* him. All she could do was remember him—who he was, what he looked like. But she couldn't see him. Therefore, she couldn't see his shadow. She didn't know if Ceyon's hand was involved in this, yet she didn't want to wait for his image to come. She knew that her consent to see Ceyon's shadow was enough. She wasn't afraid anymore, to see his full picture. His one-dimensional character had become more complex. Yes, he had his beauty, and he also had his shadow. And Tasha was willing to see it, without fear.

Early the next morning, Tasha went straight to meet Lee. She didn't want to wait. She was ready to face Ceyon and felt that she must free herself from him. She wanted to love.

Lee was waiting for her. He took her to a bridge, and while they were standing there, he said, "A bridge has two sides. If you are on one side, you can't be on the other. But if you are on the bridge, you can be on both sides at the same time. By that, you are able to transcend time and space."

"How does it lead me to freedom?" Tasha asked.

"It would grant you the liberty to act according to your wishes, regardless of physical limitations, in any given situation," Lee replied. "This kind of freedom, to be able to be in two places at once, allows you to make decisions that transcend the existing boundaries, unleashing within you a creative force."

"So is being in two places at once my next step?"

"Your next step," Lee answered, "is to transcend your perceptions of what is possible. You will achieve it by creating a bridge and learning how to be in two places at the same time.

"Now go back to the town. If you see two sides, two places, and you want to be in them both, look for a bridge. It is always there. And if you don't see the bridge, create it in your mind. Imagine it and it will be there."

"Would my body actually be in two places at once?" asked Tasha.

"While you are in two places at the same time, your actual body remains at the place you are, before using The Bridge technique. Your experience at the other place will be real and alive, as if you were actually there. You'll be able to talk with people, and people will see you as if you were truly there. Yet when this experience comes to an end, you will find yourself back in the place from where you started it all."

"What would happen if someone touches my actual body?" Tasha asked.

"Then your experience will be stopped, and you will return to your body at once. But you can start it over again when you wish."

Then he said, "Go, Tasha, and look for a bridge and come back when you find it."

On her way back to town, Tasha felt a strong wish to see Lia again. She wanted to visit her, yet she didn't want to leave town. She didn't want to go back to Lassa. She remembered Lee's words: "There is always a bridge. And if you don't see it, create it in your mind." So she looked for a bridge that could take her to Lia's place, while at the same time staying here.

What will be the bridge? she thought, and then said, "Nula's soup." Both women had nurtured her and given her the food she needed.

So she went to Nula's restaurant and asked for soup. She imagined the soup becoming a bridge, and, suddenly, she found herself in Lassa, in the front room of Lia's inn. It was empty, so she waited for Lia. Memories of the place came back. She remembered those days and nights in bed, and Lia's kindness. And she remembered the pain.

Then Lia came in. She had changed. Her face was tired, as if she had lost her great vitality.

Tasha walked toward Lia and said, "Hi, Lia."

Lia was surprised to see her. "My dear Tasha," she said. "When did you arrive? I didn't notice the door opening."

All Tasha said was, "How are you, Lia?"

"Since you left, Tasha, I haven't received even one visitor. No one comes to this inn. It's as if the place has been cursed. But if this is the price to pay for your health, I would do it again. I'm so happy to see you. Come, I'll make you some soup."

They ate the soup together, and Lia told Tasha that Ceyon had visited the house only once more. He took his things and never came back. He was the last person to step into the inn.

"I'm happy to see you, Tasha. I'm so happy that you are well. Your eyes are shining," Lia said. Then she continued and asked, "Have you met Ceyon again?"

"Not yet," Tasha replied.

Lia didn't ask more questions. Like always, she showed respect and kindness to Tasha.

Tasha felt Lia's vitality returning, as if she were remembering who she was, who she wanted to be.

Tasha hugged Lia and said to her, "Dear Lia, live your life. Dare to live your life. You taught me that, and you were a good teacher. I must go now. Open the door, and let the sun shine again on your lovely inn. I'm sure that you'll have some visitors soon. Open the door, Lia, and I'll go through it to my journey."

"I would love to do so, Tasha. I'll open the door for you. Don't forget to stop in a town named Solla and find Dara." Then she continued, "Go to your future, Tasha, to your life. Go, my child, and know that I will always love you."

Tasha hugged her, said good-bye, and went away.

Tasha found herself back in Nula's place, and her body was shivering. Then she heard Nula say, "Tasha, your soup is cold. Do you want me to make you a fresh one?"

"Don't bother, Nula," she replied. "Your soup was delicious, as always. But I must go now."

She left Nula surprised, next to the full bowl of soup. Nula shook her head as if saying, *This Tasha is special. Although I don't always understand her, I love her very much.* Then she took the bowl and went back to the kitchen. After all, it was another busy day, and she must go back to her work.

34. STEP FIVE: DARE TO LOVE

The Laughter

Tasha returned to Lee. She knew that he saw the bridge in her eyes.

He said to her, "Dear Tasha, you're almost ready to face Ceyon, but in order to do so, you must learn the fifth step: Dare to love. It's easy when you cannot see the shadows of people, but now that you can see the shadows, you must dare to love. I can't say another word about it. I can't instruct you or explain it to you. Dare to love, and you'll be ready to meet Ceyon. Now go, Tasha."

Tasha was confused. She didn't know where to go or what to do, so she simply walked down the streets. Eventually, she found herself in front of Ian's empty house and decided to go in. She wanted to feel the atmosphere there.

The door was open, so she walked in. Although the place was deserted, all the furniture was there, as if time had frozen. In the wardrobes she saw some clothing. Dishes were on the table. Time truly had stopped here. But she could hear laughter—it hadn't stopped. She could sense Ian's happy childhood.

Strangely, she felt at home. She felt, in a way, that she was a part of this family, of this happiness. She could hear the ocean.

She remembered the ocean in Ian's eyes and knew that it was his ocean, rather than hers.

Suddenly she heard a voice, "Hi, Tasha."

It was Ian. He was there.

Tasha spoke quietly. She told Ian that she could hear laughter and could sense happiness. She told him that she could hear the ocean. Her heart was naked and her hands were bare. She was very vulnerable at that moment, and yet, she had never felt such happiness before.

Ian came closer and looked into her eyes. All he saw were those endless meadows of hers. Tasha was endless in this moment, and he could sense it.

"Do you hear the laughter?" she asked him.

"I can't stop hearing this laughter," he said. "To you it's happy music, but to me it's a nightmare."

"But this laughter is real, Ian. It's not an illusion. So how did it become a nightmare for you?"

"Since *that day,* I have been longing to hear the happiness in the laughter again. But it isn't there for me."

"Be quiet, Ian," Tasha said gently. "Listen to the laughter. It is here for you. It is here for us. Just listen to it."

Ian listened. Suddenly, his face became softer. He became vulnerable as well. But he couldn't bear it and turned to go.

"Don't go, Ian. Don't go yet. I love you."

Ian turned and looked at her. He looked at her as if she were the only person in the world, as if she were the world. Tasha saw it. Ian came closer, and Tasha said, "Ian . . ."

But Ian put his finger on her mouth and said, "Let's respect the silence and the laughter, and our laughter."

And he kissed her lips. Tasha felt the sweet taste of it. But it wasn't just sweet, it was also bitter, as if Ian's shadow had entered this kiss. It was sweet, it was bitter, it was life.

Tasha knew that her love for Ian was real, but she also knew that the time to face Ceyon had come. She wanted to be with Ian, and she would stay with him for the whole day. But at first dawn, she must leave and go to the unknown.

When the night came, Tasha told Ian that tomorrow she must go, that she must face her empty house. "But I will return. I promise you that."

Ian didn't say much. All he said was, "Go, Tasha. Go and face the spirits haunting you. I'm here and I'll stay here."

In the morning, Tasha went to say good-bye to Lee. But neither Lee nor his house was there. She remembered Lia telling her to look for Dara in a town named Solla, on her way to the ocean. But even before this, she knew that she had to go back to Belle to find the man who talked to her at the gates. His resemblance to Ian was so strong that she had to find out who he was. She felt that he wasn't only the key to Ian, but the key to Ceyon as well.

Although feeling the pain in leaving Ian, Tasha knew that she had to go again to the arms of the unknown and face her past. Her life was waiting for her. And now her love was waiting for her, too.

PART III

THOSE OLD CODES OF THE PAST

35. A DIFFERENT TOWN

So Many Empty Houses

After a few days, Tasha reached Belle. Instead of the lively town she remembered, she was surprised to find the streets empty. Instead of the shining sun, the atmosphere was cloudy, though there wasn't one cloud in the sky. She found the place where she had lived, and the sign "The Precious We" was still there. When she went in, everything seemed the same as the day she had left, as if time had stood still. *Was it Ceyon's hand?* she thought to herself.

Tasha saw a group of young people standing together. Although she hadn't met them before, she walked toward them and greeted them.

They looked at her and asked, "Who are you?"

"I'm a visitor, but I used to live in this town. What has happened here?"

One of the young people said, "There was a storm, a desert storm so strong that some people lost their lives, and some lost their belongings. After it passed, many decided to leave. Our town isn't *Belle* anymore."

Tasha looked around and didn't see any signs of the storm.

"But the houses look the same. I can't see any trace of a storm."

"We restored everything," one of them said. "We worked hard. The outside appearance looks perfect, but if you go into the houses, they are empty. It may seem as though the storm has passed, but it's still here."

So many empty houses, she thought. *One of them is mine.*

She asked them if they knew a place for her to stay for the night, and they told her that no one had visited the town since *that day.* "But try Lynn's," one said. "She might help you." They showed her the way, and she thanked them and went straight to Lynn's house.

Lynn was a thin woman, gentle in her posture. When Tasha asked for a room, Lynn took her to a small room and only said, "I'll call you for dinner." Tasha saw that Lynn's eyes were kind, yet she sensed that Lynn was avoiding speaking to her.

It was a small room without much furniture. Everything was modest and clean, like Lynn.

When Tasha entered the main room for dinner, she saw a big table filled with food. Lynn said that she was waiting for her friends to join them.

Tasha offered to help, but Lynn invited her to sit, and told her, "You are my guest, my first guest since *that day,* and this is a blessing."

After a while, there was a knock at the door, and two young couples entered the house. Lynn was proud to introduce them to Tasha.

When they all sat down to eat, Lynn, looking at Tasha, said, "May this lady be our blessing. We need visitors. We need people." She couldn't say anything more, as if she had become emotionally overwhelmed.

One of the women said, "It's all right, Lynn. This is a special day for you and all of us." Then she turned to Tasha and said, "Thank you. You have brought hope to our town. Let's raise our glasses to a new beginning."

One of the men poured wine into the glasses and made another toast. Tasha looked at them and saw that the shadows of the people of Belle remained the same as they had been before the storm—they still felt lonely. Belle hadn't faced its shadow yet.

Tasha blessed them with happiness and friendship, and they ate their dinner quietly and peacefully.

In the morning, Tasha thanked Lynn for her kindness, and asked to pay for the night.

And Lynn said, "Don't pay me. I owe you more than you know. Go, young lady, and may the angels guard you."

Tasha thanked her and went on her way. She had to leave Belle and knew her next stop would be Solla to meet with Dara. On her way out of Belle, she looked for the man at the gates. She wanted to talk to him, but he wasn't there.

I know that you belong to my story, Tasha thought to herself. *We are going to meet, even though I don't know when or how.*

36. DARA

North Became South

It took Tasha only a few days to reach Solla. It was a town with paved streets, fancy stores, and some small farmhouses on the outskirts.

She asked her feet to take her to Dara's house. When she reached the place, it was locked and no one was there. Tasha prayed that empty houses wouldn't haunt her again.

She sat on a bench next to Dara's house and waited. She thought about Ian. She remembered the ocean and their kiss. Sweetness and bitterness were interwoven into one fabric of life. She wanted to live, she wanted to love, but she must face *that day.* She must do it. There was no other way.

She fell asleep and was awakened by a touch on her shoulder. "Hello," she heard, "are you waiting for me?"

Tasha saw a tall and graceful woman. In a way, she reminded her of Lia.

"Are you Dara?" Tasha asked.

"Yes, I am. Come in."

They entered the house. It was a nice home with a big yard.

"I'm Tasha. Lia asked me to visit you."

"Yes, I know. Please have a seat."

Dara sat next to her and then asked, "Where are you going, Tasha?"

"I'm going to meet Ceyon."

"Are you ready?"

"I know that the time has come," Tasha answered. "But I don't know if I'm ready. Time will tell, not me."

Then Dara continued, "What are you taking with you to this meeting?"

Tasha waited awhile and then said, "I'm taking the courage to see. I want to be free, Dara."

"Aren't you already free?"

"I know that my prison isn't real, but it is my reality," Tasha answered. "My freedom is real, but it's not my reality."

"You are a wise young woman," Dara said. "I can see that you've trained your heart, and that you want to experience true love. And I can see that you genuinely want to be free. But let me tell you what I also see. You want to meet Ceyon, believing that after this meeting, you'll be free. However, if Ceyon is the key to your freedom, the key remains in his hands. Tasha, Ceyon is not the key—he is only a door. Are you willing to see that?"

Tasha didn't say a word. Yes, she had thought that after meeting Ceyon, she would be free to live and love . . . but what if that was merely an illusion? What if, as Dara said, Ceyon was *not* the key?

"I must go, Tasha. I'll be back later on," Dara said. "Take your time and think about it. You can stay here as long as you'd like."

Tasha didn't know what to think. All that she had done was to prepare herself to face Ceyon, but now she was left with questions that pulled the ground out from beneath her. If Ceyon wasn't the key, who was? If she was the key, why couldn't she simply open the door? What was the door to freedom? What was the door to love?

Tasha felt the struggle again. She wanted to talk with Ian. She wanted to touch the ocean again. When she looked into Ian's eyes, she didn't need a key. There were no fences or walls. She wanted to use The Bridge technique in order to talk with him, but she knew she shouldn't do that. Ian couldn't rescue her from her journey.

She didn't know what to do, think, or feel. She was in complete chaos. North became south, and east became west. Tasha had lost her compass. She didn't know which was the right way to go anymore.

Night fell on the town. Tasha felt as if a deeper darkness had penetrated Dara's house. She decided not to struggle. She was ready to let go and be free. She sat at the table and wrote a letter:

> *Dear Ceyon,*
>
> *Everywhere I go, I see you. You've become my haunting spirit, and I've become yours. If I can see you everywhere, you can see me everywhere as well. Come and face me. I am the key and the door to your freedom.*
>
> *I know that you can see me, and I know that you can see yourself. Come and meet me. I'm ready to set you free. I'm ready to be free.*
>
> *Tasha*

Tasha put the letter on Dara's table and left the house. She knew that she must go back to Belle. If those empty houses were hers, then they were Ceyon's, too.

37. LYNN

Too Free for This Town

Tasha reached Belle a few nights later and went straight to Lynn's house. Lynn welcomed her. She didn't question Tasha, as if she were used to the unpredictable currents of life.

"Stay here as long as you like," said Lynn. "My home is yours."

Tasha thanked her and went to her room. She knew that she wouldn't leave Belle until she had faced Ceyon. She didn't know when he would come, but she knew that he would.

In the morning, she walked down the street but didn't see any familiar faces. The people were all new to her, even though not even a year had passed since she had lived here.

Then she saw Sol, one of the women she had met at the dinner at Lynn's house. They greeted each other warmly.

"Tasha," Sol said. "I thought you had left."

"I did, but I just returned."

"That's good to hear. Lynn must be pleased to have your company."

Tasha asked, "You seem very close to Lynn. Does she visit you often?"

Sol paused and then replied, "No. We love Lynn, but after the storm, she became reclusive. She doesn't leave her house much."

"What happened to her in that storm?"

"It's not a good time to talk now, as I must be going. But please come visit Lou and me tonight. We live very close to Lynn's house. Ask her to show you the way. Good-bye for now, Tasha. We'll see you later."

When it became dark, Lynn showed Tasha the way to Sol and Lou's house. "Enjoy your evening," she said to Tasha. "I'll be here."

When Tasha entered their house, she smelled delicious food. Sol invited her to the table. "We were just going to have dinner. Will you join us?"

"I'd be glad to," Tasha said.

Sol and Lou were friendly and made her feel comfortable. Tasha asked them to tell her Lynn's story.

Sol said, "Lynn was a unique woman. She didn't live by 'the rules.' She did only what she wanted to do. She was a free spirit. Her speech was eloquent; her posture was graceful. She didn't want to get married or have children. She was generous and kind to so many people, encouraging them to follow their hearts. Some said that she had crossed the line, and many were jealous of her. And some people, like us, adored her. We still do."

Then Lou said, "She was alone in her house when the storm came. Lynn tried to close all her windows but didn't succeed. It was too windy and came on too fast. She choked and fainted.

"We didn't know if she was going to survive, but she slowly returned to life. However, her ability to communicate was damaged. She doesn't leave her house much now or visit with people as often as before."

Sol continued, "Some people say that she deserved this punishment, that she was too free. But others think, as we do, that she is still a free spirit. Maybe when she lost consciousness, she saw some things about life that changed her. Maybe she knows more than we realize.

"Anyway, we love and appreciate her. Lou repaired her house after the storm. From time to time, as you saw, we enjoy visiting her and having dinner together. If she said that you are a blessing for this town, I'm certain she knows what she's talking about."

"Where were you when the storm came?" Tasha asked.

"We were here," Lou said. "But we have a cellar, and we passed the storm quite well, although our home was damaged."

And Tasha continued, "So many people lived here before—where did they go?"

"We don't really know," Sol replied. "They simply went away and spread to the four winds. They couldn't stay here, not even for one more day."

"And what about you?" Tasha asked.

"We love Belle," Lou replied. "We were born here. We have friends here. We didn't want to move. And besides, you can't run away from storms. The storms will find you. Won't they, Sol?"

"We don't want to run away, Tasha," Sol said. "We want to live here. This is our place."

They continued to talk for a while. The atmosphere was pleasant and peaceful.

After dinner, Sol and Lou took Tasha back to Lynn's house.

And Sol said, "Come again, Tasha, whenever you wish. If you are a blessing for Lynn, you're a blessing for us, as well."

Tasha thanked them and went in.

Tasha saw Lynn sitting on the sofa and felt much love toward her.

"How are you, Tasha?" Lynn asked.

"I'm fine. Thank you for introducing me to Sol and Lou. They're very kind."

"Yes, they are. Good night, Tasha. I'll see you in the morning."

Tasha went to her room. She thought about Lynn, about her losing consciousness, about the dramatic change she had gone through, and how the storm had shown her no mercy. *We are all the same, aren't we?* she said to herself. *When the storm hits us, we are changed dramatically. And from that day we are not the same anymore.*

She thought about Ian, and wished him goodnight.

38. THE MAN

Full of Presence, Yet So Elusive

Tasha had already been in Belle two weeks. Lynn was very kind to her, yet didn't keep her company. Lynn didn't want to talk much and seemed content with her life. Tasha saw Sol and Lou a few times. They were always kind and friendly, but they had their own lives.

Each night, before sleep, Tasha remembered the empty houses. She remembered Ian. She remembered Ceyon. And she knew that she was not going to leave this place until she met Ceyon. He would come at the right time, as always.

In her dreams, Tasha saw the image of Ceyon. But it was an elusive image. It had its presence, yet it was untouchable. So was Ceyon himself. So was her life. Full of presence, and yet so elusive.

During the day, she would take walks around the place. The valley was still beautiful, although it too had changed its colors, its mood, its atmosphere. A shadow was there, mixed with the beautiful scenery. This was the story of Belle. But it was Tasha's story as well. Shadow and beauty danced inside and outside of her.

One day, when she returned from one of her walks, Lynn told her that a man had come to see her. She had invited him to stay and wait for Tasha's return, but all he said was, "I'll be back."

Then he disappeared, as if he had vanished.

"It was strange," said Lynn. "I might even have imagined it."

"No, you didn't imagine it," Tasha replied.

Tasha saw that Lynn didn't want to continue the conversation. So she thanked her and went to her room. Although Tasha knew that Ceyon always came at the right time, in her eyes, he remained unpredictable. She couldn't foretell his steps or his moves. He would be back, but when, was up to him.

The days followed each other. There was no trace of Ceyon. A week went by, and Ceyon still hadn't arrived.

Lynn didn't ask Tasha about the man she had seen. This was Lynn's nature. She respected one's journey. Lynn was different from Lia, yet they were so alike. They saw people as they were. They saw their shadows, and they weren't afraid of life or its consequences. They weren't at all bitter, although their lives had taken a different course from their dreams.

One morning, Tasha set out for the gates of Belle, hoping to meet the man who looked like Ian. She could think of nowhere else to find him. When she reached the gates, however, they were closed. No one could go out or come in. Tasha knew that Belle needed visitors and went to open the gates, but stopped when she heard a man's voice say, "Don't do that."

She turned to look at the speaker. It was him, the man she had met at the gates on the day she left Belle.

"Why do you want the gates to remain closed?" she asked.

"Because another storm is coming," he answered.

"How can the gates stop a storm from coming?"

"The world is more than you can see."

"Still, how do you know that a storm is on its way?" Tasha continued.

"I know things," he simply said.

She moved closer toward him and asked, "Do you remember me? Do you remember the day that I left Belle?"

"Yes, I do."

And she continued, "Who told you to say those words to me?"

"No one," he answered.

Tasha looked into his eyes and saw a small boy happily running in the fields. And she dared to ask, "Who is the boy in your eyes?"

The man was surprised, yet remained silent.

"Who is the boy?" Tasha asked again.

"Why do you care?"

"Because this boy is in great danger," she answered.

Suddenly, Tasha saw pain in the man's face. But the pain passed swiftly, and he said, "Don't worry. You should go on your way."

Tasha looked at him very carefully. She didn't know why she had thought he looked exactly like Ian. They shared somewhat of a resemblance, but a few months ago, she would have been certain that they were the same person. And now he looked quite different.

Did the storm hit him, too? she asked herself. *Did he lose his impressive appearance because of the storm?*

"Please tell me your name," Tasha asked.

"You can call me the Man," he said.

"My name is Tasha." She offered her hand, but he didn't respond. It was as if he were in another place.

"I must go now," Tasha said, "but we'll meet again. I'll come and help you keep the gates of Belle in the face of the coming storm."

The Man, who was quite serious, burst into laughter and said to her, "We can make a good team together, can't we?"

Tasha laughed back and asked, "When do you expect the storm to arrive?"

"Soon," he answered. "Very soon."

"Do you want to warn the people?"

"Not yet. Maybe together we can keep the storm out of Belle. I know that you have some powers, and I have mine. Perhaps we can do it."

Surprised, Tasha looked at him, wondering, *How did he know about my powers?* Yet all she said was, "Yes. Perhaps we can."

The Man didn't say another word and walked away without saying good-bye. Tasha noticed that he was both here and there at the same time. It was as if he didn't belong to any one place, as if he had no roots, as if he were a drifter without his consent.

Tasha didn't tell Lynn about the coming storm. She wanted to give their powers a chance to keep the storm out of Belle.

The image of the Man followed her. Although he could go wherever he wanted, he was loyal to keeping the gates safe, but she didn't know the nature of this loyalty. Was it an act of free choice, or was it his prison?

Another day passed, and Ceyon didn't return.

39. THE STORM

Take Care of Yourself

Tasha was awakened that morning by the sound of the coming storm. She got up and without any hesitation or delay went directly to the gates.

The gates were open, but the Man wasn't there. She tried to close the gates, but they were stiff. It was as if they were very old, as if no one had touched them in a long time even though they were closed yesterday. Tasha heard the storm coming. Its voices were very alive. She couldn't hear any mercy in them. Deep in her heart, she asked the Man to join her, yet she was on her own. She stood between the open gates, as if trying to keep the storm away with her own body.

If someone has to face the storm, she said to herself, *it would be me.*

The storm was getting closer and closer. You could see the dust and hear the roaring sound. Tasha turned and looked at Belle. She saw the empty houses, the deep loneliness and the longing eyes of the people who wanted to live and love. Then, she turned back to face the storm.

Suddenly, she shivered. She turned around and saw Ceyon. He was standing at a distance. She couldn't see his face, only his form. He beckoned her with his hand, as if saying, "Come. Come to me."

Tasha was between the gates, facing a storm in front of her and a storm behind her. She knew that she didn't have time to hesitate. At that very moment, the people of Belle were more important than her own private journey. Ceyon could wait. The people of Belle couldn't. Their lives were at stake.

She turned to face the storm, knowing that Ceyon was behind her. It was a strange feeling. She had been waiting for this moment for so many days, and here it was. Yet the moment offered her an entirely different situation. And she chose. This moment would not be given to Ceyon or to her. It would be given to the people of Belle.

Tasha could see the storm right in front of her. It took everything that was in its way. Nothing remained still. The leaves, the trees, the bushes, the stones, the sand, the desert—all came toward Belle. *In a few moments,* Tasha said to herself, *the storm will try to take me as well. The storm will try, but I can try, too.*

Then a thought occurred to her. *Perhaps the storm has a shadow. Through its shadow, I'll know what to do.*

As she looked at the side of the storm, she saw something that surprised her: tenderness. *What a strange sight,* Tasha said to herself. *This ruthless storm, which took upon itself to be so inconsiderate and cruel, has a tender shadow.* She had never thought about tenderness as a shadow before. Then she looked at the storm as if it were a huge pet that needed a warm caress and some loving words.

"So many people want to live, want to love," Tasha said softly. "And you, Storm, cannot help them do so. So you need to go away. Go to where you belong." She sensed that the storm didn't like its tender side, but continued, "Go home, Storm. Go to where you belong. Take care of yourself."

And the storm suddenly became a small ball, which Tasha caught in her hands. She held it with great care and love. When she looked into the ball, she saw a struggle—as if the storm didn't like its new shape but at the same time liked the soft touch of her hands. For a moment, Tasha wanted to take it with her, but remembered that this tender ball could destroy the town. So she sent the ball to the four winds.

When she turned back, Ceyon wasn't there. He had disappeared. Tasha knew that she hadn't faced the real storm yet.

On her way back to Lynn's house, Tasha thought about Ian. He was so far away, yet so near. *I know that love must be simple,* she said to herself. *Yet how can one love with so many voices inside him?*

Then Tasha remembered the image of Ceyon, how he had waved to her, beckoning her to come. *The storm is not over,* she said to herself. *It is not over yet.*

40. FREE SPIRIT

Those Old Codes of the Past

Lynn was home when Tasha entered the house. She told Tasha that she'd heard the sound of an approaching storm this morning. Although the sound stopped, it seemed that a storm was on its way. "Perhaps another storm is needed to give the people of Belle a real chance to live," she said. "The first storm left a horrible memory in everyone's mind. Sometimes by facing a second one, people can set this memory free and bring life back to their homes and to this town."

Tasha couldn't remember Lynn initiating a conversation since she had met her.

"Maybe the sound of the storm is enough," she said to Lynn. "Maybe the people of Belle don't need another storm in order to restore their hearts."

Lynn looked at her and said softly, "Maybe you're right, Tasha. Perhaps we don't need the whole storm, and the sound of it is enough. If so, we are lucky."

Lynn spoke as if her spirit were set free. Her speech was fluent and eloquent. *Lynn was indeed lucky,* Tasha thought. *She didn't need the whole storm. The sound of the storm had been enough for her.* But it wasn't enough for Tasha. She must face the storm in its entirety; she must face Ceyon.

Then Lynn said, "Let's go out. It's a lovely day. I want to show you a very special place."

Yes, Lynn was free, and it was a beautiful sight.

Lynn had taken Tasha out of town, to a small hill from which you could see the whole valley.

"Let's stop here," Lynn said. "I want to tell you a story."

They sat down on a bench, and Lynn continued, "I wasn't born in Belle. I was born in a small village in the desert, where you could see dunes of sand and beautiful sunsets. The people in my village were hard workers. They didn't have time to look at the sky, to count the stars, to chase the clouds. They looked at the ground all day long. They wanted the ground to bring them food.

"But I knew that the sky could bring us food as well—and they didn't like it. To them, I was a dreamer, and they wanted me to be a worker like them. But Tasha, I wasn't a dreamer. When I looked at the sky, my feet were rooted in the ground. Yet, I must admit, I wasn't a hard worker. I didn't believe it then, and I don't believe it now.

"The hard worker doesn't have time to live, to love. I don't know if the people in my village even knew that there are stars in the sky. So when I reached the right age, I left my village, my family, my parents. My presence didn't help them live their lives like they wanted to. In a way, they were ashamed of me. I was born a woman, and as you know, there is a well-defined code for what it is to be a woman. But I didn't fit this code in their eyes. So, I left the village and came here to this valley.

"Look at Belle from here. Isn't it a lovely place? Look at the valley, the green meadows. Isn't it beautiful? I helped build this town. I wanted it to be a place of free spirits. I wanted the people to live their deepest wills, their deepest wishes. But although it's a valley and not the desert, the people who came to Belle brought the defined codes of their pasts with them. They wanted a fresh start, but they didn't want—or maybe were afraid of—a fresh spirit. So they started to imprison their utmost dreams. And suddenly, they became hard workers.

"I tried to take them on a different course, but gradually I was left alone. It was as if I were too free for this valley as well, as if someone could be too free. I understood that a change of place could merely be a change of outward appearance. If people aren't willing to take a risk to be free, the old, defined codes will haunt them over and over again."

Lynn paused for a while and then added, "I look at you, Tasha, and I see your free spirit, but I can also see the old codes in you. You still let these codes govern your life. I don't know what you should do. To be free means that you cannot base your life on other people's ideas. It depends only on you. It's not a mission, and it's not an assignment. It's whether you want to be free or not. You still have the codes of your past haunting you. I saw your past. He knocked on my door twice. I only told you about the first time. But when he came, I knew that this was your past. The second time was this morning."

Tasha was surprised, yet she remained silent. Yes, she must face her past. And Ceyon was her past. Lynn saw through her and said it very clearly: Those old codes of her past were still haunting her.

Lynn and Tasha sat there on the hill, surrounded by beautiful scenery. This was only the outward appearance, however. Inside Tasha, the scenery was very different. But she wanted to change it.

"Let's go, Lynn," Tasha said. "The third knock on the door is usually the last, and I must be there."

Lynn hugged Tasha and said, "Come then. What are we waiting for? Let's go now."

41. THE SHADOW

Heavy Burden of the Past

Tasha stayed at Lynn's house and waited for Ceyon to return. He came at night. When Lynn heard someone knocking, she knew that she must open the door rather than Tasha. And he was there.

Ceyon said that he wanted to see Tasha. Lynn asked him to come in, but he replied, "Thank you, but I prefer to stay out here."

Lynn went to call Tasha. Tasha had heard the knock on the door, and she was ready. She didn't know what she was going to do or say. All she knew was that she couldn't carry the heavy burden of her past anymore.

When she reached the front door, Ceyon wasn't there. She went outside, but he wasn't there, either. And then she saw him at a distance, waving his hand as if saying, "Come. Come, Tasha."

Tasha walked toward him silently. When she reached the place he had been, she saw him again at a distance, waving his hand as if inviting her to follow. So she continued to walk toward him. It was a dark night. Tasha felt the chill, but took a moment to look at the stars to remember her own free spirit.

When she reached the place he had been, Ceyon again wasn't there. And again at a distance he waved his hand, inviting her to follow him. But Tasha sat down. She didn't say a word. She just sat down, and that was all. She remained there for a while and couldn't see Ceyon. His presence was all around her, yet she couldn't see him. Eventually, she decided to go back to the house. She got up, and when she turned to go, Ceyon was standing there. He was so close, so near, that she could hear his heart beating, but she couldn't see his face clearly.

"Hello, Tasha," Ceyon said. "It has been a long time since we last met."

Tasha didn't answer.

"How are you?"

Tasha still didn't answer. She just stood there in front of him.

Ceyon stared at her. Tasha knew that he was trying to look right into her, but she had put up a veil. She wasn't an open book to him anymore. She couldn't see his eyes, but she knew that he could see hers. Slowly her eyes would adjust to the darkness, and she would see his eyes as well—and she would also see his shadow. So all she did was stand there, without a word.

"You wanted to see me. You asked me to come and meet you," said Ceyon. "Here I am. What do you want, Tasha?"

Tasha remained silent. She wanted to see Ceyon's shadow first. She didn't need to see his face in order to do so. She only needed to look at his side. Then, suddenly, she started to see his story, her story.

She saw herself sitting in the mud *that day*, calling for help, asking for Ceyon. She saw that she had fainted, and Ceyon hadn't come for her. He had heard her call, he even saw her, but nevertheless, he didn't come. She knew that he hadn't helped her. She had already seen that when she was at Lia's place, but she didn't know why. Why hadn't he been there for her?

Then she saw the Man near her, in the mud, on *that day*. He had been there. He had brought her back to the gates of Lassa. Who was he? How had he followed her? It had been a rainy day, and no one had been there. Why hadn't Ceyon come and helped her? Then, she saw the orange. The image was so strong. She saw the jealousy. Still, why hadn't Ceyon come for her, even if he had been touched by jealousy? The Man picked her up with great care and took her back to Lassa. And Ceyon, her teacher, her guardian, had left her to die. Suddenly, she couldn't see anything anymore. And Ceyon wasn't there. She looked around, but he had disappeared.

She went back to Lynn's house. She wanted to tell her what had happened, but Lynn said to her curtly, "No, Tasha. Don't tell me yet. It's for you and for you only. Otherwise, it will be my story, too. Tell me when you decipher the codes of your past, but not before. It's for your sake and my sake as well."

Tasha wished Lynn goodnight and went to her room. What had happened on *that day*? Why hadn't Ceyon, her teacher, been there for her? Why had a stranger, a man she had not known before, come to her rescue? Must she wait to see Ceyon again in order to unfold the real story? She felt that she couldn't be dependent on Ceyon's comings and goings. There must be a way she could reach him without leaving this house. She would find the bridge. But now, she must sleep. It had been a long day, a very long day.

42. THE MASTERS

Not One of Our People

Tasha woke up early in the morning. She still wanted to see the full story, but before that, she wanted to talk to Ian. She didn't want to tell him her story and make her story his. But she did want to see the ocean again—to feel at home for a moment. She didn't want to leave Lynn's house, so she would create a bridge and meet him right now.

What could be the bridge? There was no ocean nearby, and she didn't want to go to one of the empty houses. Then she remembered the coin she had found inscribed with "A DATE FROM GOD." She looked for it and found it. It was a small coin, but God was there, and Ian was there, too. She looked at the coin and found herself near Ian's house. She didn't want to go inside, so she sat there and waited. And Ian came.

He was surprised and happy to see her. He hugged her and asked, "Tasha, what are you doing here?"

"I haven't finished my journey yet," she said, "but I wanted to see you. I wanted to see your face."

Ian hugged and kissed her. There was no need for words.

After a while, he looked at her and said, "Tasha, you must go. There is a dark cloud hanging over you. I love you. I love you very much, but you can't stay here."

Tasha knew that he was right, but she needed a few more moments of this love.

Yet Ian, as if hearing her, said, "Sorry, Tasha. You don't have those moments. You must go."

"But, Ian . . ."

"You must go, Tasha. Go. Go now."

She felt an ache. She wanted to stay, but she knew that Ian was right.

Then, she found herself back in her room, in front of the small coin. Lee had trained her so that she could face her past. She knew that to set herself free, she must see what had happened, and she didn't have time to waste.

She thought, *What would be the bridge to Ceyon? An orange or potatoes?* She chose potatoes. She found some potatoes in Lynn's kitchen and took them to her room.

Then she looked into the potatoes and saw Ceyon at Elijah's house. Ceyon was there alone. She wanted to look at his side, without his knowing it. Otherwise, he wouldn't let her see what had happened. So she decided to stay afar and look at him from where she was.

She saw, again, how the Man had brought her to the gates of Lassa. But she wanted to see where Ceyon had been at that moment, on *that day,* and there he was, meeting with the Masters of the Shohonks. They were talking about recruiting more children who were born to be Shohonks. They looked into the names of the children, as if the children were there in front of them. Name after name, name after name. For them, the names were real children. Through the name, they could see the child. They talked about how hard it was in those days to collect the children from their parents. It was as if the word *Shohonk* had lost its value, its respect.

Nevertheless, they said, these children would be collected. Nevertheless, they would be recruited.

And then Tasha heard a voice, *her* voice, pleading for Ceyon to rescue her. She wasn't the only one to hear it. Ceyon and the Masters heard it as well.

"Are you going to help her?" one of the Masters asked him.

"We are in a middle of a crucial meeting," Ceyon said. "I can't leave now. The decisions of this meeting will affect our people's lives."

So the Master said, "Maybe she is not one of our people, but you were her teacher."

Ceyon paused and then said, "I took it upon myself to take care of her, and I know that her journey is special. Yet this time I trust Mother Nature to help her. I trust that she will be safe."

The Master looked at him. Although Tasha couldn't see his face clearly, it seemed that he hadn't liked Ceyon's answer, but they had crucial decisions in front of them, and they continued with their meeting.

Then Tasha saw the Man next to them. He wasn't a master. He was a simple Shohonk who knew how to keep the gates safe. He was a guardian who knew how to guard. He had heard Tasha's voice. He had heard Ceyon's words. And he went to help her. He was Mother Nature's angel. Tasha remembered how Ian had told her that Mother Nature's angels had raised him. Perhaps this person was one of them.

But that didn't really matter right now. All that mattered was Ceyon's choice. He hadn't been there for her. He was there for his people, and she wasn't one of them.

She found herself back in her room. Then she heard a knock on the door, and Lynn came in. She told Tasha that she shouldn't stay in the room all the time. "You are not a prisoner, Tasha. You can't wait for Ceyon to come back. Let's go out. It's a nice day."

Tasha looked at Lynn and asked, "How do you know his name?"

"I simply know, Tasha," she replied. "And stop being amazed. When you are free to see, you can know many things about life, about people, and even about names. Stop being haunted. I am not your enemy."

Tasha looked at her. Yes, she admitted to herself, for a moment she thought that Lynn was one of Ceyon's messengers. Yet Lynn didn't belong to anyone, only to herself.

"I'll come with you," Tasha said.

"Let's go, Tasha," Lynn replied. "You are free to go wherever you want. I once told you that you are a blessing, and you still are. Let's go now."

43. THE GATES

Unspoken Gratitude

Tasha followed Lynn. She followed her until they reached the gates of Belle. The gates were open, and Tasha was surprised by how easily Lynn closed them. When she had tried to close the gates, they had been so stiff. And now, they moved easily in Lynn's hands.

"Why do you close the gates?" she asked Lynn.

"Because I want you to open them."

"But they were open."

Lynn insisted, "Yes, but it wasn't you who opened them."

Tasha looked at Lynn. It seemed that Lynn knew more than she had said. "Open them. Open the gates, Tasha."

Tasha opened the gates, but they immediately closed. They didn't stay open.

Lynn said, "Open the gates, Tasha, but not for only a moment. Open them so others may pass through them."

Tasha did so. She opened the gates with firm intention, and took her hands off them. And they stayed open.

Then Lynn said, "Come and sit next to me for a while."

Tasha was sitting next to Lynn when she heard a voice say, "Hello. How are you?"

She looked up and saw the Man standing there.

Tasha got up and said, "Oh, it's you! I'm fine, and how are you?"

"I'm fine, too," he answered.

"You weren't here when the storm came."

"No. I couldn't come," the Man answered.

Tasha looked into his eyes and again saw the little child running and playing. "Why couldn't you?"

"I just couldn't," he said, turning to leave.

"Don't go yet. I want you to meet a dear friend of mine." She turned to Lynn and said, "Lynn, I want you to meet someone."

Lynn got up and greeted the Man.

"This is the man who keeps Belle's gates safe," Tasha continued.

"What's your name?" Lynn asked.

"I prefer to be called the Man," he answered.

Then Lynn said, "But you are more than that."

The Man looked at her surprised, as if asking Lynn, "What do you mean by that?" But he didn't say anything.

Lynn continued, "If you keep our gates safe, you are more than just the Man. You must have a name."

Tasha was surprised, too. She didn't understand what Lynn meant.

"Why is knowing my name important to you?" the Man asked.

"Yesterday, I heard the storm coming," she said. "The sound of it was the same roaring sound as the last storm. I heard it, and then suddenly it stopped. If you keep our gates safe, you're more than just the Man."

The Man looked at Lynn. "No, you misunderstand. Yesterday, it was her," he said pointing at Tasha. "She was the guardian. I wasn't here."

Lynn looked at Tasha, "It was you?"

"Yes," Tasha replied.

Lynn looked at Tasha and said, "It's good to know that you kept our gates safe. It is a true help." Then she continued, "And you, young man, don't hide behind a gray veil. Find your name, and you'll be free."

The Man looked at her. "Thank you," he said. "But life is more complicated than you think."

"Yes, life is quite complicated," Lynn replied. "But one cannot use that as an excuse for running away from who he is."

Tasha looked at Lynn. Lynn didn't give up when she saw a chance for a free spirit.

"Dear woman," the Man said, "I can see that you are straightforward in your words, and I can see your courage. But I think I've found my own way in life. With your permission, I must go."

When he turned to go, Tasha suddenly realized that she had forgotten to thank him for rescuing her on *that day*. But he wasn't there anymore; he had just gone away, and she was left with her unspoken gratitude.

"He is a special man," said Tasha.

Lynn looked at her. "Yes, he is, but you are special, too."

They went back to Lynn's house. While they were walking toward the house, Tasha saw Ceyon. She shivered. She hadn't expected him to come in the daytime, without knocking at the door. Lynn saw that, but didn't tell Tasha what to do. She just stood by her.

She looked at Tasha as if to say, *Tasha, you must trust yourself. You must trust your name.*

Tasha hugged her and went toward Ceyon. Lynn didn't stay. It wasn't her story. It was Tasha's.

Ceyon sat on a bench, and Tasha sat beside him. All she said was, "You didn't come to help me *that day.*"

Ceyon didn't say a word.

"You chose not to help me," Tasha continued. "You knew that I could die, yet you chose not to be there for me."

Ceyon sat quietly, but not peacefully.

Then Tasha looked at him and said, "You made your choice. And it wasn't me."

She saw a struggle in Ceyon's face. He tried to put up a veil, but the struggle was too strong. Suddenly, she saw the child that she had seen in the eyes of the Man. It was the same child. And she said straight out, "The child is in great danger, isn't he?"

Ceyon was surprised, yet he didn't reply. He looked at her. Her eyes were innocent, but she wasn't blind anymore. She could see. And she could see through him.

"You asked me to come and meet you," Ceyon then said. "Why?"

Tasha looked at him and said, "Years ago, I met a man with a free spirit, whom I trusted, whom I loved. But gradually, he changed, and I didn't know it. I was blind, a naïve child. And when he made his choice and didn't rescue me, I became his prison. His guilt haunted him. He sent his messengers to the four winds to make me lose my senses so that I wouldn't haunt him any longer, but in a mysterious way, with the help of Mother Nature and her angels, I regained my senses. The walls of his prison tightened around him. It is you, Ceyon—it's not me. I've never haunted you."

Ceyon didn't say a word. He couldn't discern any trace of hatred or anger in her voice. For a moment, the sight of Tasha was too bright. He couldn't bear it, yet he remained sitting.

"You made your choice, Ceyon," Tasha continued, "and you have to face it. Your shadow penetrated your life. It is for you to face, not for me. I have my own life to live. I don't have the time or the will to haunt you. I don't like your choice, but it was your choice, not mine. Stop sending your messengers. I've let go of you. Can you let go of me so that we can both have a fresh tomorrow?"

Ceyon didn't answer. It was as if he wished to have time for himself. Tasha left the bench with him still sitting there. She didn't know what he was going to do. All she knew was that they would meet again.

44. A WONDER

The Dimension of the Shohonks

Tasha went straight to Lynn's house, but she wasn't there. Tasha felt empty, yet she sensed no sadness within her. She was calm and peaceful. She didn't hear thoughts or opinions. She was vacant, as if preparing a place for a fresh tomorrow.

She decided to meet with Elijah again. Elijah had wanted to tell her a few things, but it hadn't been the right time for her, back then. Now she was ready to hear them. Tasha left a note for Lynn, telling her that she must go and that she would come back soon.

"Don't worry," she wrote, "I remember my name."

Tasha asked her feet to take her to Elijah's house. When she reached the place, Elijah didn't seem surprised. She welcomed Tasha in and asked her to sit down. Tasha told Elijah she was ready to hear what she had once wanted to tell her.

"Dear Tasha," Elijah began, "I know Ceyon, but I'm not his messenger. I am his friend. We were trained together to be Shohonks. Ceyon was a wonder, a special boy. The masters loved him, although they saw his shadow. And you have met his shadow. You have been hurt by it. But deep inside, Ceyon loves you."

"Does he?" Tasha asked.

"Yes, he does. It's just that he also envies you. And do you know why? Because he can't see a trace of his shadow in you.

Moreover, he scarcely sees any shadow in you. Your only shadow was your inability to see the shadows of others. And when you began to look at others' shadows, your own started to disappear. However, don't underestimate the challenge that is ahead of you. To trust and love people despite their shadows is not a simple task at all."

"I've tried to move on in spite of what happened *that day,* but the prison is still here," Tasha said.

"I'm not telling you to move on with your life, Tasha. I don't know what is right for you. I had wanted to tell you about Ceyon's shadow, but you discovered it on your own, at your own pace. Each of us has our own timing.

"Yes, you are Ceyon's prison. You gave him a chance to be free again, but it's not over yet. Life is more complicated than it appears. Ceyon is your prison, too. And you know it. But now it's a good time for a good meal."

As they ate together, Elijah told Tasha her story, about the price she had paid for the path that was chosen for her. And she told Tasha about her yearning for true love.

Then she said, "You weren't born to be a Shohonk, Tasha. You were born to reach the ocean, to experience love. Go and live it. You may pay a price, but it will be worthwhile. You are stuck in the dimension of the Shohonks. You must leave this dimension behind you; otherwise, you'll see Shohonks everywhere. That's not your journey. It's not your path. Lead your life. Be in touch with people. Get attached to them. Dare to love, Tasha, and may Mother Nature's angels be with you."

45. GREED

A Teacher and a Child

Tasha had expected to see Lynn when she returned to the house. She wanted to tell her about her conversation with Elijah, but the door was open and Lynn wasn't there. Tasha didn't want to stay inside, so she went out.

Dear Ceyon, she called him. *Find me wherever I am. Please come now.*

She went to the hill where Lynn had taken her and sat there. The view was beautiful, and everything seemed so serene, yet Tasha didn't feel that way. She felt excitement. She felt some fear. She wanted to be free, but what did it really mean to be free?

She looked at the view again. The houses of Belle seemed so beautiful and lively, but she knew that loneliness dwelled inside them as well.

I want to touch the real world, but what is real? she asked herself. So many thoughts circled inside her. She felt the prison. It seemed so real.

Then she heard a voice from behind her say, "Tasha."

She turned and saw Ceyon. He was standing very close to her. And suddenly, he was the teacher and she was a child again, a ten-year-old girl who gave her hand and let Ceyon take her to the unknown. She got up but didn't say a word. She knew that Ceyon saw through her, and she didn't want to put up a veil. She didn't want to struggle. She was vulnerable at that moment, yet she let it be.

I can't fight anymore, she said to herself. *I simply can't. The fight is over.*

Ceyon saw her vulnerability, and in it, he also saw her profound strength and beauty.

"Tasha," Ceyon said. "What do you want me to do?"

"Nothing," she replied.

"I heard your call," he continued. "So I came. What do you want?"

"When I looked at you, I thought you were a true free spirit. Now I can see you are human, as we all are. Still, I want to be free, but suddenly, I don't know what it means."

"Tasha, the wish to be free could become a prison. 'I want to be free—freer than ever.' This is not freedom. This is greed, which leads only to suffering and misery."

Tasha looked at him and saw his sincerity. "But how can one let go of greed?"

"I don't know if I can show you that."

"You can try," she replied.

Tasha didn't know what was going on in Ceyon's mind. Suddenly, the veil was there, but she didn't give up.

"Ceyon, this is our chance. Our chance, not mine alone. There were many times when I wanted to be a Shohonk. It seemed like a noble way of life, to be beyond attachments. This was my prison, and in some extent, it still is. You are a Shohonk who has remarkable powers. But it wasn't enough for you. This was your prison, and in a way, it still is."

Some time passed before Ceyon replied. "Tasha, I've always appreciated your honesty, but life is never that simple."

"You don't need to accept my words," Tasha said, "but don't reject them. I don't hate you. I am a person who wants to live and love, yet you're constantly trying to prevent me from doing both."

Tasha looked into Ceyon's eyes. She wanted to see his depth, but the veil was there. She knew that no matter what he might say, the existence of the veil showed fear. She had given up her veil.

She had given in. She couldn't be afraid anymore. She couldn't let fear conduct her life. Yet Ceyon, her teacher, was still using the veil.

So she asked, "Why do you need the veil? I won't harm you, and you know it. Why do you still need it?"

Ceyon didn't answer her question. All he said was, "Tasha, there are things for you to learn." And he turned to go.

"Don't go," she said. "You're not living alone. We still live together. It's too easy to sneak off at night without saying a word. You told me that people with inner strength always speak out. I'm not an obstacle in your life. I'm a person. So please don't go."

Ceyon turned back and said, "I must go, Tasha, but I'll return." And he went on his way.

Tasha was left standing there alone on the hill, surrounded by the view of Belle, and she felt empty. She felt lonely. After all, she wanted to live; she wanted to love. She didn't want to run away. Not anymore.

46. A RIDDLE

The Man Without a Name

Tasha went to the gates of Belle to meet the Man. They had never spoken about *that day* he had rescued her. He had been there for her and hadn't asked anything in return. Tasha felt great admiration for him. He was humble. However, perhaps he was too humble, the man without a name.

And the Man was there, next to the gates, as if he was waiting for her. Tasha asked him to follow her, and he agreed. When she found a nice place, they sat together.

"Dear Man," she said, "I know that you rescued me *that day,* and I want to thank you, but I don't know whom to thank. Your name is a riddle—a secret that you hold on to. I don't want to invade your privacy, but I've learned that there is no such thing as privacy. We are all connected. You heard my voice, you heard my call, and you came. It wasn't a private conversation. The Masters heard it, too. I'm sure that you've heard many calls throughout your life. But can you hear your own call?"

The Man looked at her. "Don't try to rescue me, Tasha. You don't owe me anything. I heard your call and wanted to help you. I didn't need to do so. I didn't do you a favor, so you don't owe me anything."

Tasha looked at him and said, "I know that as a Shohonk, you stay detached from close relationships, as if you need a safe distance to keep you away from risk. I respect your path. I respect your choice. But what about friendship? I can't be your friend without knowing your name."

"I'm not a riddle, Tasha," he answered. "I'm not a victim or a martyr. I'm a human being who tries to do his best, to follow his own path. I'm a simple man, whose life was chosen for him. Since I was a child, I've tried many times to run away from my destiny, but time and time again, an inner voice forced me to come back, to follow this road. I am your friend, yet I can't offer you friendship in the way you define it."

Tasha looked at him closely. She saw honesty, but she also saw pain. Because of the pain, she continued, "And do you still want to change your path?"

"Tasha," he answered quietly, "you're still trying to rescue me. Don't do that. Go to your life. Make friends. Enjoy your path. Remember, you won't enjoy your own path if you insist on walking along other people's."

"But I can see your pain," she said. "I see a child, a lovely child, in your eyes over and over again."

"Yes, you see that. But the story is mine, not yours. When you see other people's stories, try not to feel them. Otherwise, you'll get stuck in them. Now you're in my story, and you're trying to solve it, as if my life is a problem to be solved. Live your life, Tasha. Don't make your clear sight a curse. You see people—their beauty and their shadows—and it's wonderful, but after seeing that, you must dare to love.

"You are attracted to Shohonk people, but we can't offer you the love you want to experience in your life. We can't become attached to people through close relationships. I am your friend, but you must go and find another kind of friendship. Otherwise, you will feel lonely and empty."

Tasha felt much love for the Man and wanted to hug him, but she respected his wish for distance.

Then she asked, "Do you think that one day you'll be able to tell me your name?"

He looked at her and paused for a moment. "I don't know, Tasha. I really don't. Now go to your life. It's waiting for you."

47. THE WIZARD

Dare to Fly

When Tasha returned from the gates of the town, she met Lynn walking down the street. *Lynn looks so vibrant,* Tasha thought to herself. *Yet she keeps a distance from people.*

So she asked her, "Do you think that a free spirit always keeps a distance from others?"

Lynn wasn't surprised when she heard Tasha's question. "Tasha, you think too much. I can't answer this question because there isn't a right answer. Stop thinking. Stretch your wings and dare to fly. The wind will take care of you." Then Lynn began to walk away.

"Where are you going, Lynn?"

"You don't need me, Tasha. You must continue alone. You have all you need, and my presence won't help you."

"What do you mean by—"

"Stop thinking," Lynn interrupted. "Stretch your wings, Tasha. I'll see you later." And she walked away, leaving Tasha on her own.

Everyone sends me back to myself, Tasha thought. *It seems that I don't understand the real meaning of it, because the message keeps knocking on my door.*

Tasha was near the bench where she had met Ceyon. She understood that she couldn't go in circles anymore, so she sat down.

"Dear Tasha," she heard a voice behind her saying. "May I join you?"

It was Ceyon. Tasha moved aside to make room for him.

But Ceyon said, "Come, Tasha. There's a place we have to go, both of us. This is the right time to do it. Follow me."

They reached a place outside of town, where a stream was swiftly flowing. "Look at the water, Tasha," he said. "So much water. Do you think that the desert envies the valley?"

Tasha looked at him and said, "No, it doesn't. It loves being a desert."

"But look at the water. So much fresh water. Don't you think that the desert is cursed?"

"Nothing is cursed."

"I belong to the desert, Tasha," he continued. "And you belong to the valley. You belong to the water. Did you know that?"

"I haven't thought about it," she answered.

"Do you know what my name means?"

"No, I don't."

"*Ceyon* means 'wizard of the desert.'"

"That's beautiful." Tasha said.

"There are times that I don't find it beautiful. Wherever I go, the desert follows me. Wherever you go, water follows you, whether it's a stream, a roaring river, or an ocean. You are the one who is going to reach the ocean, and I will stay in the desert, no matter where I go."

"What's wrong with the desert?" Tasha asked. "I love it."

"There isn't much life in the desert. People need water in order to live. I'm the wizard of the desert because I can create water from out of nowhere, but it's my creation. It's only my creation. Wherever you go, Tasha, you'll find water—you'll find life. Aren't you lucky?"

Tasha looked at him and said, "I don't know whether I'm lucky or not. Not too long ago, I wanted to be you. I wanted to create water from the vast expanse of sand, but gradually, I understood that this wasn't my true will. To live and to love, truly love despite the shadows, is my creation. So I don't know if *luck* is the right word. Each of us must follow his own way. I must follow mine, as you must follow yours."

Suddenly, she felt deep love toward him, and he saw it.

"You're a brave woman," he said.

Tasha knew that he was brave to say that.

Then he asked, "Where are you going from here, Tasha? You are a beautiful woman, and you are brave. What are you going to do in the coming future of yours?"

"My love is waiting for me," she answered.

"Yes, but what are you going to do?" he asked again.

"I don't know. All I know is that I always seek freedom and true love, and I'm willing to go again toward the open arms of Nowhere, until the day I reach the ocean."

"So go on your way, Tasha," Ceyon said. "I'm not your prison anymore. You're free to go. The ocean is waiting for you."

He stood next to her. He was silent, at peace. When she looked into his eyes, the veil wasn't there.

Suddenly, she could see Ceyon's beauty again. She could see his strong wish to be a man of dignity and integrity. She could see it clearly, but at his side, she saw much shame. He was ashamed of his shadow.

"Before I go," Tasha then said, "I wanted to ask why you sent your messengers to haunt me. I've tried to forget my past, wishing to be free, and then the messengers arrived—the lady in the lace and Sid's father. Why?"

Ceyon remained quiet for a while and then said, "They were never my messengers, Tasha. They were yours."

Tasha looked at him with great surprise.

"I never haunted you. Your will to be free summoned all these messengers to push you toward the arms of your true freedom. They were Mother Nature's angels in disguise who came to shake your world so that you would remember your own sacred wish for friendship and love. They came to remind you that unless you are free, you wouldn't be able to experience the genuine meaning of togetherness. It was your request that set things into motion, not mine."

Tasha was overwhelmed. She sensed the truth in Ceyon's words. When she looked at him, she saw the person she had once known—the man who was honest and worthy of her trust.

Then she remembered that some of the messengers she had met along her way indeed arrived as if they'd heard her call. Elijah and Lee told her that. But what about the lady in lace and Sid's father?

She could see now how she had tried to create a sense of togetherness in Belle, and yet remained alone. "Your past is still alive, too alive," the lady had told her. "You must go back to the desert and face your past." *So it was me,* Tasha thought to herself. *It was my deep wish to be free, which set forth all that has happened since I moved to Belle. The people around me echoed the words that helped me know I was imprisoned. Some shook my world, and some offered guidance and a sense of home.* She thought about Lee, Nula, and Lynn. *They were my messengers rather than Ceyon's.*

Tasha was quiet. She needed time to grasp the flow of what had taken place in her life. She needed to think about the enigmatic nature of reality, of what had seemed so real just moments ago.

She looked at Ceyon and said, "I didn't know all of that."

"But now you know," Ceyon said gently.

"Now I know," Tasha said quietly, as if to herself.

The sight of Tasha at that moment was a blend of genuine sincerity and deep strength. Ceyon sensed that her inner being found peace.

"Why didn't you tell me that before?" she asked.

"Because only now it can truly serve you."

She looked again at Ceyon and saw his love for her, and yet the shame was still there. She wanted to ask him why he didn't come for her, but it wasn't the right time for that. She decided to leave this question aside for the moment and move on with life, her life.

"Dear Ceyon," she said, "I'll go now. I don't know where you're going from here, but all I want to say is . . . *love the desert.* Love its strength, its beauty, its benevolence. Yes, the desert has its dark side, but who doesn't? I loved the desert, Ceyon. I still do."

They stood there for a while, as if they needed this time to remember who they were.

When Tasha entered the house, Lynn was sitting on the sofa. She looked at Tasha and said, "It's time for you to go."

Tasha wanted to tell her about the meeting with Ceyon, but Lynn wouldn't let her. All she said was, "Tasha, you don't need to tell me anything. I can see that you're free. You are a free woman. You must go, and you must go now."

"But, Lynn . . ." Tasha started.

"Tasha, you can't stay here any longer. Don't become attached to your past. In a way, I've already become your past. Take your things and go. I'll send your regards to Lou and Sol."

Dear Lynn, Tasha thought, *she never gives up when she sees a chance to set the spirit free.*

Tasha went to gather her things. She didn't have much to take with her. After a while she returned, hugged Lynn, and thanked her.

All Lynn said was, "Thank you, Tasha, for coming. You are a blessing. I hope you will remember that. Go and spread your blessing. You are filled with love, young woman. Go and give it. Good-bye, Tasha."

They hugged again, and Tasha went on her way. After all, life was waiting for her and so was her love.

PART IV

FROM ASHES TO ENDLESS SKY

48. REFLECTION

Follow Your Path

Tasha reached the town by nightfall and went straight to Nula's restaurant. Nula was happy to see her.

"You've changed, Tasha," she said. "You became a woman, and you're even more beautiful. Give me just a moment, and I'll come and sit with you."

Tasha sat at her usual table, and when Nula joined her, she asked about Ian.

"He left town a few weeks ago," Nula replied.

"Where did he go?"

"I don't know. Ian never says where he's going."

Tasha sat silently, not knowing what to say or do.

When she went to the hotel that night, she remembered telling Ceyon about her willingness to go toward the arms of Nowhere. It was now that she felt the true meaning of it.

Tasha woke up the next morning, and in spite of the coldness of winter, she wanted to go outside.

When she left the hotel, Ian was there, waiting for her. Although surprised, she walked toward him slowly and gracefully. She was happy to see him. They stood there hugging each other.

It wasn't a time to talk. When Tasha looked at Ian's face, she saw pain mixed with happiness.

"When did you get back?" she asked.

"Just now," he replied.

"Where did you go?"

"I went to see my brother."

Tasha was surprised. Ian never mentioned that he knew where his brother was, but all she asked was, "And how is he?"

Ian didn't answer. It seemed that it was too painful for him.

"Let's take a walk," Tasha suggested.

They walked until they reached the place that was always green.

They sat next to the water, and Tasha said, "Do you remember when you told me about looking in the clear, still water and seeing your reflection? The clear water is here. Do you want to see your reflection?"

"I know what I'm going to see," Ian answered.

"Try. Look into the water," she said. "It may surprise you."

After a long pause, Ian looked into the water. Then he said, "I see a small boy playing in a field."

"Do you know this boy?" she asked.

"It's me, when I was young, not long before my family disappeared." Then he said, "Tasha, I don't know if I can be a good friend right now. You're a beautiful woman. I can see that you are free, but I still have many things to figure out in my life."

Tasha looked at him and said, "I don't know what life holds for us. All I know is that I want to be with you and to live with you. So, let Mother Nature and her good angels help us. We are not alone. I'm here, and you're here. That's all that is important."

Ian hugged her warmly. "Tasha, I don't know if you really understand the full meaning of what you've just said."

"I don't, and I might never know, but I can't let this lack of full understanding rule my life," she replied.

They sat quietly next to the water, simply enjoying each other's presence. After a while, Ian told Tasha that he must leave. He must go back to see his brother.

"But you've just arrived," she said.

"Yes, I know, but I have to go again."

"When will you come back?" she asked.

"I don't know, Tasha."

Tasha looked at him and said, "Follow your own path, Ian. Go to your brother. Let's see what will come."

Then she continued, "How did you find your brother?"

"I didn't. I went to meet him, but he wasn't there."

"Where will you go now?"

"I'll continue to look for him until I find him, although I don't know how long it will take me. Be free to go wherever you want, Tasha. Please don't wait for me."

Tasha hugged him and kissed him good-bye. "Go, and may Mother Nature and her angels be with you. I will be with you as well. Take care of yourself, Ian."

He hugged her again. "Good-bye, Tasha," he said and went on his way.

Tasha walked back to town to see Nula.

"Hello, Tasha," Nula said, "come in and sit. Have something to eat."

But Tasha replied, "Nula, I want to speak with you."

"I'm listening," she said.

"I'm leaving town, and I don't know if I'll be back. I want to thank you for being who you are. This town is lucky to have you. I was lucky, too."

"Where are you going, Tasha?"

"I don't really know," she replied. "But I must go. There are places waiting for me, and people I am waiting for. I'll find my way."

Nula looked at Tasha. "Dear Tasha, of all the people I've met, I can tell that your path is different. Your beauty and strength are a gift. I would love for you to stay here, but I know that this is not the right place for you to live and love. I want you to know that wherever you go, I'll be there for you. Please, remember that.

Sometimes it helps. I bless you, my child. To me, you will always be a child."

Tasha hugged Nula and left the restaurant. She felt empty, although it wasn't a sad emptiness. It was just emptiness.

49. LAMAR

Sweet Dreams

Tasha let her feet take her wherever they wanted to go. Days passed before she reached a big village. She noticed that the gates of the village needed care. No place that respected itself would be proud of such gates. Tasha passed through them and entered the main street. She sensed sadness and heard a cry of despair. She decided to stay the night and looked for an inn, but nothing she saw seemed nice. It was as if the people of the village had given up on beauty.

Tasha entered a small café to ask for a hot drink. It was wintertime and quite cold. She looked around, trying to figure out what had happened to this village.

A young woman who worked there approached her. "What's the name of this village?" Tasha asked.

"Lamar, which means 'sweet dreams,'" the woman answered. "You're new here, aren't you?"

"Yes, I am. I've just arrived," Tasha replied.

"Where will you stay for the night?"

"I don't really know yet."

"Stay with me."

Tasha looked at her. She was young, in her mid-twenties. It was as if she wanted to live, but despair was already in her eyes.

"Thank you," Tasha replied. "I'd be glad to. What's your name?"

"My name is Nadia. And yours?"

"I'm Tasha."

"I'll see you later then, Tasha," Nadia said. "I finish work in about two hours. I'll wait for you outside the café. You can stay here, or do as you like. I'll see you later." And off she went.

Lamar. Sweet dreams, Tasha thought to herself. *Where are they?* She decided to have a look at the village. She was interested to know what had taken the sweetness from this place.

There were people in the streets, and they looked sad. It wasn't due to hard work or a weary life. They were just sad, and Tasha didn't know the reason for that. Still, she could sense a spark of life in the midst of all this sadness. It seemed as if this village had once been very lively and happy.

When Tasha returned, Nadia was waiting outside the café.

"Let's go," Nadia said.

She took Tasha to her house. It was a small house, yet there was enough room in it.

"What happened to this village?" Tasha asked.

Nadia looked at her and said, "It's a sad story, Tasha. I'm not sure you want to hear it. There is a lot of pain in it. You're only a visitor, and I recommend that you stay a visitor."

"I still want to hear the story."

"I usually don't tell it to strangers," Nadia said, "but you don't seem like a stranger, although I can't explain why." Then she continued, "Two years ago, five children from the village disappeared in one day. They were all boys around six years old. It was as if lightning had struck our village. Since then, the village hasn't recovered, and it gets worse each day. The grief is everywhere. You must understand that we were like one big family. It was a terrible day."

Tasha could see tears in Nadia's eyes. "Did it touch you personally?"

"My brother was one of the five boys who disappeared," Nadia said. "Actually, they didn't just disappear—they were kidnapped."

"Who did it?" Tasha asked.

"Please, I don't want to go into it," Nadia replied.

"Were they Shohonks?"

Nadia looked surprised.

"It's not only your story, Nadia. It's also mine."

They didn't talk much afterward, as they both needed time to be alone. The house, although it was small, enabled them to be together and alone at the same time.

I'm free, Tasha said to herself. *These are not the walls of my prison. I'm not stuck in the dimension of the Shohonks anymore. Yet they are a part of my story, and I can't remain indifferent to what is happening. I don't know what I'm going to do, but I can't remain indifferent. I've met the Shohonks, and I know about the complexity of their world, but Nadia doesn't know anything about them, except their actions. She can't talk with them, but I can. They can't kidnap children. They simply cannot do it. They are still a part of my story, and it's for me to try to help.*

When Tasha woke up in the morning, she went to say good-bye to Nadia, but she was still asleep. She left her a note, wishing that one day Lamar would live its sweet dreams once again and so would she.

50. SACRED PURPOSE

Awe and Wonder

On her way out of Lamar, Tasha stopped at the gates, asking the Man to come and meet her there. She remembered how he had said they made a good team, and she needed his help. He was very close to the Shohonk Masters.

To her surprise, he heard her and came at once.

"I'm sure you know what happened to this village, *that day,* two years ago." Tasha said.

"Yes, I do," the Man replied.

"I know that I can't rescue people from their lives, but I can't stay indifferent, either. The Masters of the Shohonks use their power in a frightening way. They've forgotten who they are. I would like to speak with them. Can you take me to them?"

"Tasha," the Man said. "The Masters strongly believe in their deeds and act with a sacred purpose. I can't see a way for you to reach them."

"I'm sure we can find a way. We must find someone within the Shohonks, someone who can see the difference between what is real and what only seems real."

"The Masters have a great fear of extinction, Tasha. They are afraid that without doing these deeds, no matter how cruel they seem to be, the Shohonks will disappear from the face of the earth. The one who experiences such fear has no rules or limitations."

"What about the children who were taken without their parents' consent?" Tasha asked. "Why don't they do something?"

"They adapt to their destiny, but they are filled with pain," the Man answered.

"Why do they accept that their destiny is forever sealed?"

"You don't understand," the Man replied. "The power of the Masters is immense. They evoke awe and wonder in their deeds, in their words, in their lives. The children are recruited when they are very young, so gradually, they accept their fate."

"As you did?" Tasha asked.

"Yes, as I did."

"I can't accept the notion of a sealed destiny. I want to do something to help those children. You know what it means to be taken from your family—you know the taste of that pain. I'm not looking for an innocent world. All I want to do is to talk. Maybe my words will open a new door. I must give it a real chance. Will you help me?"

"If you're going to do this, Tasha, you must do it right. Otherwise, your deeds will be merely blind and naïve, and it will all be in vain. I've lost my childhood, and I don't try to get it back anymore. I'll help you, not for my sake, but for the other children. However, you must promise me not to try to save me from my destiny again."

"I promise," Tasha said and smiled.

"We can't do it alone. We'll need more help. I would like you to meet one of Mother Nature's angels, but not now. Go to a town named Shole, and I'll meet you there tomorrow morning."

The Man went away, and Tasha went on her way to a new town, to a new day.

51. LEO

Not an Outsider

Shole was a large town with its many streets, many people, and many houses. Tasha found a room for herself in a small hotel.

In the early morning, the Man arrived and asked her to follow him.

"Come, Tasha," he said. "I want you to meet someone who's going to help us. But first, I want you to hear what he has to say, and only then make your decision about whether or not to go on with your plan."

They reached a house on the outskirts of town. It was a plain, simple home. The Man knocked on the door but didn't wait for an answer. He went in, and Tasha followed him.

The house was bigger than its outward appearance and had a large backyard with green grass.

Then she heard the Man say, "Leo, we're here."

Leo was sitting in the yard, as if waiting for them. He had a vital presence and confident appearance. He didn't rise to greet them. He asked them to sit down and join him.

Tasha offered him her hand and introduced herself.

All he said was, "Sit. Sit. You don't have time for this." Then he continued, "I've heard that you want to talk with the Shohonk Masters. Do you really understand what you want to do?"

"I can't say that I do," Tasha said. "But I can't wait until I fully understand. I want to do it. I'm not an outsider. I've tried to be, but I am not."

Leo looked at her, and Tasha felt that his look was the same as Ceyon's. He read her like an open book, and she let him do so.

"What do you want to say to the Masters?" Leo asked.

"I don't know the exact words," she answered. "But we can't allow the sadness and deep mistrust to prevail. So many children are possessed by pain. What good can come from this? How can a Shohonk whose eyes are covered with the veil of such pain have clear sight? In a strange way, the Masters eliminate the spirit of the Shohonks by trying to rescue their own people."

Leo looked at Tasha. "By confronting the Shohonk Masters, you may face harsh words, which might lead to harsh consequences. When you stir things up, an unpredictable outcome may arise. Are you ready for that?"

"Yes, I'm ready," Tasha said. "This is not a whim or an impulse. This is my true will, and I need your help."

Leo then looked at the Man and said, "She is ready. Please come tomorrow morning, and we'll talk about the Shohonk Masters, who they are and how they can be reached. I'll see you then."

When they left Leo's house, the Man said, "Tasha, take the day to think over your decision. See whether you want to take this course. You don't have to do this just because you've said you want to. Think about it, and let me know your decision in the morning." And he went on his way.

When Tasha was back in her room, she felt that she didn't need to think it over. She saw the pain in Nadia's eyes, in Ian's eyes, in the Man's eyes. So much pain that was all in vain.

I would like to have a peaceful life, she said to herself. *I would like to have time for love. Although it seems like two different paths, in a strange way, I feel that meeting with the Shohonk Masters has something to do with my life and my true love.*

Tasha was going to talk with them. She would come with a naked heart and bare hands. This was her power, and she was ready to use it. She was ready to live her life with no hesitation or delay.

52. THE MASTERS

Four Realms, Four Winds

The next morning, Leo was in the yard, waiting for them to join him.

"I understand that you are going to do this," Leo said to Tasha. "You are going to talk with the Shohonk Masters."

"Yes, I am."

Leo looked at her and said, "We're going to help you, but you must understand that you'll be there alone when the time comes."

"I understand," Tasha replied.

"Let me tell you about the Masters and who they are. One of them you know, but the others are new to you."

And Leo continued, "There are four Masters of the Shohonks, and each has his own realm. Four Masters, four winds. Each Master has unique powers. Ceyon is the Wizard of the Desert, the Master of the South; and he knows how to create anything he wants out of nothing. He is the Master of Creation. Tor, the Master of Knowledge, the Master of the North, has access to any information he wants. Life, people, and nature are an open book for him. Then there is Kedem, who is the Master of the East. He is the Master of Shape and Form, and knows how to transform outward appearances. He is a virtuoso and takes it to a form of art. And then there is Emor, the Master of the West, the Master of the Word. He turns words into outstanding manifestations. Through words he can also influence people's minds and hearts. He is the most powerful Master. He cares about the Shohonks and their future, yet he is also strongly motivated by the lust to rule. When the Power of the Word is in the hands of such a Master, the outcome can be devastating."

It was the first time Tasha heard that Ceyon was the Master of the South—and that he was one of the four Masters. And she loved that thought.

Then she asked, "How can one Master be more powerful than the others?"

"Because the four winds are not alike," replied Leo. "Each wind has its own strength. We like to think that they're equal, as it calms our minds, but it isn't so. Years ago, the power of the North was stronger than the others. This changed, but it doesn't matter why. All that matters is that you see reality as it is."

"They are not equal in their powers, but do they think alike?" Tasha asked.

"No, not always," Leo answered. "They were all trained together to be Shohonks. They are friends and rivals at the same time. They don't always think alike, but they do share the fear of extinction, and they understand that they're dependent on each other."

"I understand their powers," Tasha said. "And I understand that they share the same fear, but what are their shadows?"

"It will be up to you to see their shadows when you meet them," Leo replied.

Tasha looked at Leo, "You are a Shohonk as well, aren't you?"

"It's not important," he said. "My story is not yours. Hold on to your own story. It will help you in the coming days." Then he added, "Your next step is to meet some of the Shohonks who were taken by force at an early age. We can do that, can't we?" Leo looked at the Man.

"Yes, we can," the Man answered.

"I want you to talk with them, Tasha," Leo continued, "but don't tell them your plans. Talk to them, ask questions—whatever you want to know."

Then Tasha said, "If there are Shohonk women, I would like to meet them first."

"There are a few," said the Man. "We'll spread the word."

"Good-bye, Tasha," Leo said. "I'll see you at the right time. Now you must go."

While they were walking back to town, the Man said, "Don't do anything until you hear from me. I'll get in touch with you, in one way or another. Just wait. Will you do that?"

"I'll wait," Tasha said.

He then said good-bye and went on his way, the man with no name.

53. TIA

A Form of Art

A day passed and Tasha hadn't heard from the Man. Patiently, she waited for him.

The next morning, a young woman approached her and said, "I came to talk with you."

Her face was calm, yet Tasha felt tension within her.

"What's your name?" Tasha asked her.

"I'm Tia. But please, let's first go and sit somewhere outside of town, and then you can ask me whatever you want."

Tasha followed her until they reached a field of wildflowers. The colors were beautiful. Tia stopped and said, "Let's sit here."

Then she continued. "You wanted to speak with us, so I'm here. What do you want to know?"

"Where do you live?" Tasha asked.

"I live in a village nearby."

"And what is your vocation? What did you take upon yourself, as a Shohonk, to do in life?"

"You don't understand," Tia answered. "The Shohonks never choose a certain deed or vocation. The vocation chooses us. Mine is to be an architect of shape and motion."

"I don't really understand," said Tasha.

Tia laughed and said, "It sounds more complicated than it is, but it's not important for you to understand because it's not your vocation. It's mine."

"Are you happy?" Tasha asked.

Tia hesitated, and then replied, "In a way, yes."

"How did you become a Shohonk? Usually only men can be Shohonks."

"My brother was born to be a Shohonk," Tia answered. She paused for a moment and then continued, "But he was very sick and fragile. My parents knew that he wouldn't survive, so they tricked the Shohonks into thinking I was my brother."

"What happened when they discovered the truth?"

"All I can say," Tia said, "is that they didn't like it. But the Shohonks live by a firm rule: Once they take you, they don't give you back. When they took me, I belonged to them already, and that was it."

Then Tasha asked, "Do you have any contact with the four Shohonk Masters?"

"Yes, I do, but not directly. I was trained to be a Shohonk, so I have my own master. He is in direct contact with them."

"What is the nature of your connection with your master?"

"He is very kind," Tia replied. "He helps me take my vocation to a form of art."

Tasha remembered that Lee used the same words. She wanted to ask Tia what her master's name was, but decided not to do so. Then she continued, "Do you have friends, Tia?"

"Not in the way that you understand friendship. I have friends, but I don't have close relationships."

"Do you wish to have close relationships?" Tasha asked.

"I don't ask myself this question."

Tasha paused for a moment and then asked, "Do you meet the other Shohonks? Do you have gatherings?"

"Yes, we do," she said. "We meet twice a year, on the first day of autumn and on the first day of spring."

"What's the purpose of these meetings?"

"I'm not really sure," Tia replied. "But all of us come to these meetings. We are required to do so. Each meeting lasts three days. At the end of it, the four Masters give a performance."

"What kind of performance?"

"It's spectacular. One who has never seen it cannot imagine its awesome power. The Masters' performances are incredible."

Tasha heard Tia's words and could sense admiration in them, but fear was there as well.

"To which realm do you belong?"

"I belong to the East realm, to Kedem, the Master of Shape and Form," Tia replied.

Tasha thanked Tia and told her that she appreciated her honesty.

"Look, Tasha," Tia said, "I hope you'll use my words with great care. After all, this is my life, and these are my people." Then she asked, "Do you want me to walk with you back to town?"

"No thank you," Tasha replied. "I want to stay here for a while. I will remember your words. Good-bye, Tia, and take care of yourself."

Tasha looked at Tia as she walked away. She was thin and tall. Her appearance was gentle, but this was only her outward appearance. To one who could see, she was untamed like the wildflowers all around them.

When Tasha returned to town, she thought about those gatherings, the spectacular performances and the awesome powers of the Masters. Tia didn't know the reason for them. *I'm sure,* Tasha said to herself, *that they are not only social gatherings.* She wanted to find out more about these gatherings, and she now knew where she was going to be on the first day of spring.

54. ETHAN

Here and There

The next day, when Tasha was walking on the outskirts of town, a young man approached her. "I'm the last one for you to see," he said.

Tasha looked at him. His face had the look of a child, naïve and vulnerable.

He is only the second one that I've talked to, Tasha thought to herself. But all she said was, "I understand. How did you find me?"

"Quite easily," he replied. "Each person has his own energy pattern. That's how I found you." Then he asked, "Do you want to ask me any questions?"

"Yes, I do," she answered. "But first, can you tell me your name?"

"My name is Ethan," he replied.

"Hello, Ethan. Let's sit."

They sat on a small hill. The clouds were hanging above. It was cold, but not too cold to sit outside.

"How did you become a Shohonk, Ethan?" Tasha asked.

"One day, when I was six years old, I was outside playing with my friends. The Shohonk people came and took me with them. I didn't want to go, but they told me that I didn't have to be afraid and that my parents gave their permission. I didn't believe that my parents did it willingly, but I followed them."

"Have you seen your parents since then?" she asked.

"No. But I know how to connect with their souls. So, in a way, I meet them whenever I want to say hello."

"Is that what you do?" Tasha asked. "You know how to connect with people through their energy patterns?"

"That's right," Ethan answered.

"So if you feel lonely, you can be near the people you love even though they aren't really next to you."

Ethan didn't answer immediately. After a while he said, "I try not to be lonely."

Tasha paused for a moment and then asked, "Do you have a master?"

"Yes, I do," he said. "Each Shohonk has a master, and I have mine."

"What is your relationship with your master?"

"He is nice and kind to me," Ethan answered. "He's helping me become a master."

"Do you want to be a master?" she asked.

"I follow my journey," he replied. "And this is all that matters."

Tasha thought to herself, *He is still a child.* Then she asked, "Do you have friends?"

"Yes, I do, but not in the way in which you think about it."

"Ethan, have you met the four Masters of the Shohonks?"

"Not directly. I've never spoken with them. I've only seen them in the gatherings."

"What do you think about them?"

"I don't think about them," he replied.

Tasha looked at Ethan. "To which realm do you belong?"

"I belong to the East realm, to Kedem, the Master of Shape and Form."

"Do you like being a Shohonk?"

"You don't understand, do you? You're asking me questions that are irrelevant to my life."

Tasha saw his inner struggle and took their conversation in a different direction. "Do you know any other Shohonks like you, who were kidnapped when they were children?"

Ethan replied, "I don't know if I was kidnapped. All I know is that I was taken from my family."

"Is there a difference?" she asked.

"Yes, there is. To be taken means that your parents gave you unwillingly but accepted that your path was to be a Shohonk."

Tasha thanked Ethan. He nodded and went on his way.

Tasha now understood why this was the last conversation she was going to have. People who were kidnapped talked the same and felt the same. When you saw one, you saw them all. Although they had the appearance of adults, they remained children. She understood why they couldn't make any changes in their lives. Their hearts were still caught in their own *that day*.

Tasha wanted to see the Man, so she decided to go to the gates of the town. When she reached the gates, the Man was there. Tasha asked him to take her to Leo. And the Man did so.

Leo was waiting for them in the yard, as if he knew that she was going to arrive. "Sit, Tasha," he said.

Tasha sat down and said, "Though they are grown up in appearance, they remain children. Their free spirits are imprisoned in the Shohonk dimension. They don't have any desire to break through the walls of their prison because they don't know that they are imprisoned. They lack passion. It's as if they are both here and there, without full awareness. It's sad, Leo. It's a sad thing to see."

"What do you want to do, Tasha?" Leo asked.

"I want to talk to the four Masters. They must see what my eyes see. And I'm not even a Shohonk."

"This is the problem, Tasha," Leo said. "You are not one of their own. Somehow, you have entered a realm that you don't belong to. You were exposed to some of its shadows, and you have a strong passion to make a change. The Masters would not like that at all."

Tasha didn't reply. She paused for a while, as she didn't want to let fear penetrate her world.

Then she asked, "Leo, why the East wind? They both belong to the East. Why is this the door to the Masters?"

"I don't really know, Tasha," he answered. "We spread your request to meet Shohonk children who were taken by force to the four winds, and the two people you met came of their own free will. Let me tell you something about Kedem, the Master of the East. He is also a kidnapped child. Maybe this is a clue. Maybe not."

"To whom do you belong, Leo?" Tasha asked.

Leo laughed. "At this stage in my life, to no one. But long ago, I belonged to the North wind, to the Kingdom of Knowledge, to Tor. He was my master."

"You must know him very well."

"Too well, I'm afraid," Leo replied. "Too well."

"Why can't you lead me to Tor?" she asked.

And Leo said, "I think the answer has already been given to you."

"Are you enemies?" Tasha asked.

"No, we're not enemies. He is simply no longer my master."

Tasha then told Leo about her plan to go to the next gathering on the first day of spring. "This is my only chance to meet the four of them together. I don't know how I'm going to do it yet or what I'm going to do. All I know is that I'm going to be there."

"Follow your passion, Tasha," Leo said. "I want to give you some advice: Learn more about the Masters. It's not as simple as you think. You must learn more about them. Otherwise, you won't achieve anything. You might be at the gathering on the first day of spring, and you might even talk with them, but you won't achieve your aim."

Tasha thanked Leo and left his house by herself, without the Man. She knew where she was heading. She was going toward the East wind to the Kingdom of Shape and Form.

55. THE GATES

Constant Change

Tasha reached the gates of the East realm. To the simple eye, there was nothing but a vast meadow. The gates weren't visible, but Tasha could see them.

The shape of the gates was constantly changing, creating a magnificent show of the many shapes and forms of gates. There were gates made of gold and marble, shabby gates, gates made of water, small gates, round ones—so many colors, so many shapes, so many forms.

The gates were closed, and Tasha couldn't enter. Their constant changing form prevented intruders from coming in. It was as if the gates had the wisdom of a guardian and knew how to keep the kingdom safe.

Tasha decided to talk to them. As they were the gates of the Kingdom of Shape and Form, they must know the form of the word.

"Hello, Gates," she said. "Please open yourself for me. I must enter your kingdom."

The gates didn't reply. They continued changing randomly, but they didn't open for her.

Tasha continued, "You want to keep the kingdom safe, but I'm not an enemy. I'm a friend. Please let me in. I'm unarmed and can do no harm."

The gates didn't answer.

Tasha looked at them. When she looked at the side of the gates, she saw their shadow. The gates of the East didn't trust themselves. She saw their story. Once when a Shohonk from a different realm convinced them to open for him, he brought great destruction to the kingdom. They remembered this story and bore the burden of guilt. Since then, they never opened themselves to strangers. These gates once knew who was an enemy and who was a friend. But after *that day,* they lost their faith in strangers, and mainly, in themselves.

Tasha knew that if the gates had been able to see through her, they would have found her to be a friend, but their fear made them blind, and she must overcome this blindness. She had to change her appearance into someone they knew as one of their people. She thought about Tia. *She comes from the East,* Tasha said to herself. *They must know her and consider her as their own.* She projected the image of Tia on the walls of the gates. Then the gates opened, and she entered the kingdom.

The realm of the East seemed wide and open, yet Tasha could sense the invisible walls surrounding it. At a distance, Tasha saw two people wearing gowns. In the outside world, Shohonks never wore gowns. They never wore anything that distinguished them from others. She didn't want to attract their attention, as she hadn't come to talk with them. She came to learn more about Kedem and his kingdom, so she used the Center-Corner Existence technique and became transparent.

By being transparent, no one could trace her. Not even the Shohonks with clear sight. Her ability to be transparent was limited, however, and she couldn't maintain it for a long time. She knew she had to use her time wisely.

Tasha came close to them. She wanted to hear their conversation. They were older people, and they were talking about something that was going to happen that night. From their words, she couldn't understand what it was, but she sensed that it was important. They talked about how they were going to circle the place with candles. Because of the dark night, they needed more light than usual.

Tasha followed them to where this event would take place. She couldn't figure out what kind of event it would be, yet she sensed a tense anticipation. Tasha left them and planned to return to the meeting place later that night.

Then she found herself making her way down a long, large corridor filled with light. Off the corridor were different doors, which were made out of a translucent material. The corridor was empty now, but Tasha could sense people going in and out of the doors, experiencing different lessons.

Along the corridor, there were no signs for guidance, but she felt that a certain order existed that everyone followed. It couldn't be left to spontaneous impulse, whim, or intuition. The realm was like a large school, and Tasha wanted to meet its principal.

56. SACRED JOURNEY

Times Had Changed

That night, Tasha came to the meeting place. The Shohonks started to assemble. The two elders whom she had seen earlier entered the place and stood in the center. The children came in, and then the adults formed a circle around them until they created a big spiral. Soon a bell chimed, and they all sat down.

One of the elders said, "Dear people of the East, I bless you all for coming to this urgent meeting. We are here on behalf of Kedem, as he won't be able to attend the meeting. He has urgent things to do in order to keep us safe, but he's going to speak through his reflection. Listen to his words."

Then the image of a tall man appeared in the center. He was taller than the two elders, and his voice was deep and loud enough to be heard by all.

"My dear people," he said, "these are crucial times for all of us. Listen to me. Listen to my words.

"We, the Shohonks, were born for a different journey. We come to this journey to bring clear sight to the confused world of the human consciousness. We must face many obstacles from the outside and from within, in order to transcend and reach the higher level of Shohonk. However, the people on the outside don't understand the value of our journey. To them, we have become a menace. We are the ones who kidnap their children. They have become victims, and we have become ruthless tyrants.

"Yesterday, their leaders made a terrible decision. From now on, they're going to persecute us because we take their children, those who were born to be Shohonks. This is a black day for us. Our days and our nights will not be the same anymore. We must protect ourselves. We must act cautiously without attracting any attention.

"Because of this, we are going to change your training. We are going to teach you to be Shohonks in disguise. From now on, no one should know that you are a Shohonk, not even other Shohonks. It's going to be your great secret. Act and talk like an ordinary person. Try to avoid any encounters with others who can expose you. Taking away your freedom to live without secrets is not an easy decision, but these are dangerous times for all of us, and we must act with great care.

"Until the completion of the training, you can't leave this realm without special permission. The gates are going to be closed to all of you. Don't try to leave. The gates will not allow you. You are not in prison, although in the days to come, you may feel that you are.

"The world of the Shohonks, your world, is about to change, but this is only to protect our sacred journey. Trust me, dear people. You must trust me. In these days, we all face crucial decisions, and this is my decision for the sake of all of us. Be blessed, my people, and may all of you be safe."

Then the image vanished.

No one said a word. A heavy silence was everywhere.

Kedem's appearance was very impressive. His speech was eloquent and impeccable. He radiated power and wisdom.

Tasha looked at the children. It seemed that they hadn't really understood the consequences of Kedem's words. They wanted a father, and he was there for them. When she looked at the adults, she saw fear in them. Their lives were going to change. After this meeting, they would have to hide and live with secrets. And one who has to live in fear, burdened by a great secret, gradually loses the ability to trust.

Tasha sat there quietly. She looked at these people, at how they tried to follow their own way. Kedem was their Master. He wanted what was best for them, but did he see them? Did he really see them?

Tasha realized that the gates wouldn't allow anyone to leave the realm, yet she wished to get out. She wanted to meet with the people outside. *Persecution* was a devastating word but an even more devastating action.

When she reached the gates, she saw that their constant movement had stopped. It was as if she had reached the walls of the realm, rather than the gates. There was no trace of them.

She tried to use the Power of the Word but nothing happened, so she decided to use The Bridge technique. Although her actual body would stay within the realm of the East, she could also be outside. She wanted to be in one of the villages that were planning to rise up against the Shohonks, and she wanted to be there now.

She thought about a bridge. *Each side tries to keep his gates safe,* she said to herself. *I'll use the gates as a bridge to meet the people on the other side.*

She looked at the walls, at where the gates had been. Suddenly, she found herself in a different place. It was a small village with small gates. When she looked at what was written on the gates she saw, "Welcome to Lovelle."

Tasha waited for first light to enter the gates of the village. She wanted to speak to these people. Yes, times had changed, but they hadn't changed by themselves. People had changed them. And people could change them again.

57. LOVELLE

It Is Paradise

In the morning light, the gates of Lovelle looked different. They weren't small at all. When Tasha looked at them carefully, she saw how they had been carved with great care and love. Tasha walked through the gates and entered the village.

It was dawn, and the people were still sleeping. The houses, which were made from wood, looked as if they were taken from a fairy tale. Each had its own garden with flowers in the front. The lanes were paved; and small, carved signs took you to the common areas of the village. It was a peaceful place, and the word *persecution* didn't match this scenery.

Tasha wanted to find the leader of the village, so she asked her feet to take her to the right place. Suddenly, she stopped next to a house, which looked like all the other houses. Nothing about it was unique or special. She knocked on the door, and although the hour was early, she heard a fresh voice say, "Come in."

She entered the house, and a man greeted her. "How can I help you?"

Tasha looked at him and said, "We must talk."

"My name is Penn," he said. "What's yours?"

"I'm Tasha, and I'm glad to meet you, Penn."

Penn invited Tasha to sit down. Tasha told him briefly about the reasons that brought her here. She told him that she had heard about the persecution of the Shohonks, and that his village may take part in it.

Penn looked at her and said, "For us, our village is paradise. We poured our love on this land, and it was kind to us. We poured our love on all people, and they were kind to us. We lived in peace until the day the Shohonks came. Since *that day,* our village hasn't been the same. Three children were kidnapped. I'm not married and don't have a family of my own, but Lovelle is my family.

"That was three years ago. We decided not to do anything. We didn't want to fight, and we don't have the skills of fighters. But a month ago, the Shohonk people sent a message that another two children should join them, and this was too much for all of us. They gave us a month to prepare ourselves for the delivery. 'Delivery' they called it, as if our children were parcels.

"We don't know how to fight, yet we can't give up these two children. We don't want to persecute the Shohonk people. We haven't any desire to do so, but we're going to protect our people."

"Why don't you talk with their Masters?" Tasha asked.

"They're like phantoms, like ghosts," Penn answered. "We never see them, so they're not people with whom we can talk. I know they have immense powers and can be very ruthless. We aren't the only village that has been hurt by them. They are very persistent and never give up on one of their own. What's the use of talking with them? They are people without faces. People without families." Then he looked at Tasha and asked, "But how did this become a part of your life?"

"It's a long story, Penn, a very long story. I've never been hurt by them in the way you've been hurt. I have no family of my own, no children. I'm young. But in the mysterious way of life, they have become a part of my story. I saw the beauty of the Shohonks that none of you has seen, and I saw their shadow, as well. I'm neither for nor against you or the Shohonks. I have a strong feeling that we can stop this vicious cycle. More than that, I know that we should do all that we can to stop it, whether we succeed or not.

When a word such as *persecution* is thrown into the air, the results can be devastating for all of us."

"I'm ready to listen, Tasha. If you have any idea what to do, I'll join you. We haven't found the key. We simply haven't found it."

Suddenly, Tasha felt that someone was shaking her body. She was in the East realm again. One of the Shohonks had found her.

"Who are you?" he asked.

Tasha regained her breathing and said, "I'm a friend."

"How did you get in?"

"Through the gates."

"But I can clearly see that you are not a Shohonk. No one can enter these gates if he is not a Shohonk."

Tasha didn't respond to this. "Who are you?" she asked him.

"I am the one who keeps the gates," he answered. Then he continued, "What am I going to do with you?"

"Let me go out," Tasha replied. "If you know how to keep the gates, please let me out."

"I can't. These days the gates must be kept closed. I can't open them for anyone."

Then Tasha said, "I heard Kedem, and I heard his command. I'm not a Shohonk, but I can help you. I've heard about the persecution, and I believe that I can help. Let me go out."

The man looked at her. He saw her sincerity, her beauty, her strength. He was an old man who had seen many things in his life.

"Don't put up a veil," he said to her. "Let me see through you."

Tasha didn't fight him. She saw the face of the man. In it, she saw his wisdom and his kindness. She had to trust him.

After a while, he said, "I will let you out. You can help us more than you know. You can do it. But remember this: No matter what you see, in your heart, you must trust people. Without trust, you won't be able to help us. See clearly. Don't become attached to illusions. Yet still in your heart, despite what you see, trust people."

Tasha knew that he was taking a risk. Kedem would know about the opening of the gates, but she also knew that he was doing it because he saw in her a real chance for help.

The man created a shape of gates. Before she went out, Tasha turned to him and started to ask, "What is—"

"Don't ask me for my name," the man said. "Go, brave woman. Go on your way."

Tasha went outside, leaving the man behind her, leaving the East realm behind her. And yet she knew she couldn't leave the people behind her, whether or not they were Shohonks.

58. A PRESENT

More Than One Layer

Tasha was on her way back to Lovelle. She wanted to talk to Penn again so they could decide the next step together, but when she reached the gates, the Man was there, waiting for her.

"Don't enter the village, Tasha. You have already planted the seeds for a real chance. Another meeting with Penn will endanger your deep will. The outward appearance of this village is beautiful. And yes, the people poured much love and care on this piece of land. Don't get confused. In moments of truth, when people are in great fear or anger, their spirits are being put to a test. The same hands that created this paradise with great love, in the face of dire circumstances, could create hell. This is the elusive nature of people. This is the elusive nature of paradise. It includes its opposite. It is always there, lurking, waiting to manifest itself. Yes, Tasha, in one motion, paradise can turn into hell. Don't enter these gates. Remember, I am a guardian. This is my mastery. Trust me."

Tasha still wanted to enter the village, but she remembered what the Shohonk in the realm of the East had said to her, "In your heart, you must trust people. Without trust, you won't be able to help us."

"So what is my next step, dear Man?"

"It's for you to decide," he replied. "But it can't be to enter Lovelle. I must go, Tasha. Take care of yourself." And he went away.

Tasha looked at Lovelle from the gates. It looked like a real paradise. She still felt the temptation to enter but decided not to do so. She didn't know where to go or what to do. She didn't know how she was going to prepare herself for the gathering on the first day of spring. All she did was ask her feet to take her to the next step. And so they did.

To her surprise, she was taken back to the desert. She was in the midst of the great, endless expanse of the desert. No villages. No towns. No people. She was there alone when her feet stopped walking.

Then she heard a voice saying, "Wait for a while. Don't move on or wander. Sit down and wait."

And so she did.

A day passed, and a second day passed as well. And there she was, waiting. She knew how to take care of herself, so she was neither hungry nor thirsty. She was neither hot nor cold, although the sun was strong during the day, and the chill was merciless at night. Tasha loved the desert, despite its blunt nature. She felt at home.

When she woke up on the morning of the third day, the Man was there. And this was what he told her: "Listen to me, Tasha. Please don't ask any questions. You have been asked to wait because this is the right thing for you. This is the time for 'word of mouth.' Your wish to create true change is spreading. Don't ask me how, but your wish has reached the hearts of many people, although they don't even know you. They don't know your name or face. Remember, you have this power to touch people's hearts, and you will see the fruits of it in the future. The seeds that you are planting in people's hearts will create great manifestations someday."

The Man paused for a moment, and then continued, "Two days from now, come to Leo's house. We will meet there. Take care of yourself. Good-bye, Tasha."

And he went away once again. He never stayed.

After two days, Tasha went to Leo's house. The Man waited for her outside the door and welcomed her, saying, "Come in, Tasha."

Leo sat in the yard, as he usually did, waiting for her.

"Dear Tasha," he said, "The first day of spring is very near. Your will is strong and clear. Readiness to welcome the unknown is already yours. So is trust in people. All that you needed to do on your own, you've already done. Now is the time for you to know more about the Masters."

Then he asked, "You saw Kedem. What did you think of him?"

"He was very impressive. I could see his powers."

"This is true of all the four Masters. What did you see in Kedem, in the person himself?"

"I saw great fear," she replied. "I didn't see hate. I saw a man who wants to protect his people. I saw fear of extinction, and I know that fear cannot lead to a free spirit."

"Tasha," Leo replied, "this is also true of all the four Masters. They strongly believe that they have a just cause. They would do anything to protect their people from persecution. They will rescue them at any cost, yet achieving things at any cost is not an act of a free spirit. It is often an act of terror.

"It's easy for us to understand the danger of people motivated by hate. But when we see people motivated by fear, trying to protect their people by all means, we become blind. We are not aware of the devastating results. In a way, we even identify with them."

These were powerful words, and Tasha didn't say anything. She just listened.

Then Leo continued, "Let me tell you about Kedem. He was kidnapped as a child, but he never felt hate. He really loved people. He was born to be a master. Anger never touched his heart, nor jealousy or greed. But from time to time, he thought about his parents and felt sad. He saw their agony. Although he knew that this was the right path for him, their suffering penetrated his heart.

"Knowing that his people experienced the same pain, he did whatever he could to shield them from future hurt and became very protective. He used shape and form to build shelter. You've seen his kingdom. Although beautiful, it is the ultimate shelter with its corridors and elusive doors. His fear has led him to create a fortress. Can you see the danger in it?"

Tasha heard Leo's words. Yet she had learned along her way that sometimes, life was indeed more complicated than it appeared to be, and had more than one layer to it.

So all she said was, "I can see the challenges that Kedem has to face, and they aren't simple at all." Then she asked, "Do you think that I should go to the other kingdoms as well?"

"No, Tasha. I don't," Leo answered. "The East realm uses shape and form to protect itself, and it even protected you. The other realms won't protect you. However, you must learn more about Tor and Emor. Follow me, Tasha."

Tasha followed Leo out of his yard, and they walked until they reached the edge of a cliff. After they sat down, Leo created a large screen in front of them.

Then he told her, "The screen that I've just created needs strong daylight to work well. Here in the bright sun, you'll be able to see the images clearly."

Tasha looked at the screen, and the images had started to appear.

"This is Tor in his early days," Leo said. "And that is me next to him. Look at Tor's face, Tasha, what do you see?"

"I see curious eyes. But I also see greed for more. It is as though he wants to know more, to see more, to have more."

"Well said, Tasha. I didn't see it then. I didn't see what you easily see now. I never looked into his eyes. I saw his height, his charisma, his magnetic presence. For me, he was God. Now, look at my face in the images. What do you see?"

"I see innocent eyes, but I can see blind naïvety, as well." Then Tasha stopped.

"Don't hesitate. What do you see, Tasha?"

"I see a strong need. The need for belonging. The need for family. The need for being secure."

Leo looked at her, "Very good, Tasha. I didn't see that either. Yes, I was seeking a father. I was seeking a family. Tor was the manifestation of all that for me, until *that day.*"

Then the images stopped.

Tasha looked at Leo and asked, "What happened there? What happened *that day?*"

But Leo didn't seem to be there, and in his eyes, she could see a trace of that deep need again.

Suddenly, sitting on the edge of the cliff, she felt insecure. *How can I trust this man? Maybe he's helping me because this is his personal revenge.* Then she remembered the words of the Shohonk at the gates of the East realm: "In your heart, you must trust people. Without trust, you won't be able to help us."

The elusive nature of people, Tasha thought. She didn't want to protect herself. She didn't want to build a shelter for herself. So she continued to sit next to Leo and wait for him to return.

After a while, Leo spoke. "I can't teach you anymore, Tasha. You will learn about Emor yourself. Remember, Emor is the strongest Master of them all and his strengths derive not only from love, but also from greed for power. No matter what the outward appearance, dare to look into him. Don't be afraid. This is your chance." Then he got up and invited Tasha to follow him back to his house.

When they entered the yard, the Man was still there, waiting for them.

Leo turned to Tasha. "This is our last meeting. I have nothing more to give you. You are a strange mixture, Tasha. You have the beauty of the Shohonk, but you came for a different journey. You'll discover your journey gradually. Trust yourself, Tasha. Yes, trust people. But trust yourself as well. You are definitely worthy of trust. Good-bye, Tasha. Go on your way." Suddenly, Leo looked very old and tired.

When they left the house, Tasha said to the Man, "This was the first time that I saw Leo leave his house."

And the Man replied, "It was the first time in a long time, indeed."

"Why has he not left his house before?" Tasha asked.

"This is a long story," the Man answered. "All I can say is that as long as he was in his house, in his yard, he was safe and remained young. But when he left his house, he became old. He knew that, Tasha. He chose to do it because he wanted you to see those images, and he trusts that you can help to create a true change. Don't let his story penetrate your heart, and don't feel sorry for him. He knew what he was doing. He gave himself a present. His present was you."

59. THE PHOENIX

From Ashes to Endless Sky

It was a few weeks before the first day of spring. The winter had been mild, and the good rain brought mercy to the land. Tasha spent those weeks without doing much. She wanted to attend the gathering free to see, free to grasp, free to be. She laid aside all that she knew. She couldn't come to the gathering with the burden of great expectations. She couldn't perceive of herself as the key, the only key. She simply wanted to talk. *Hatred and suffering were not a necessity. There must be more to human nature,* she said to herself.

She stayed in a small village, and at the right time, she would stand before the four Masters. Yes, they were strong, but her will was strong as well. Yes, they had their shadows, but they also had free spirits. She would come to talk with their shadows about their free spirits. If the shadows let her in, their free spirits would emerge like a phoenix, from ashes to endless sky.

In her days and nights, Tasha thought about Ian. She wanted to see him, but she first wanted to know what it meant to be free in a true relationship.

To learn to see shadows was one thing. To love and trust people despite their shadows was another, far more challenging, thing. As if it would be a lifelong art for her to seek. *Both Ian and I have our shadows,* she thought. *So how can we maintain our real treasures and celebrate them together, in the face of our shadows and our own "that day"? I want to live, I want to be free, and I want to love. And it is indeed not a simple task at all.*

Tasha didn't sleep or eat much. She was alert, yet peaceful at the same time. She was a fascinating combination of sharp sight and soft voice, of agile movement and solid presence. She was a mixture of woman and child, of wisdom and innocence. She was willing to make mistakes, but she wasn't willing to give up her yearning for truth, for love, for being free.

60. THE FIRST DAY
OF SPRING

An Equal Among Equals

It was the day before the gathering. Tasha woke up in the morning when she heard a knock on her door. The Man was there and asked her to follow him. He would wait for her outside.

After a short while, Tasha joined him. The Man took her outside the village. On this last day of winter, it was still cold, but the freshness of spring was everywhere.

"Smell the air," said the Man. "Breathe it. Let spring fill you with its vital blossom. Dare to be a flower, Tasha. You are not a bud anymore. Let the Masters see you as I see you: brave in your deeds and sincere in your heart. Trust yourself when you're standing in front of them, come what may. Don't grant them power that doesn't belong to them. They are powerful, indeed. But you are powerful, as well. Their presence is spectacular, and so is yours. You are an equal among equals.

"You are ready, Tasha. Take your things and go to the gathering. Remember, the Masters' appearance is always at the end of the third day, but you must be there from the first day. Know that when the Shohonks feel safe, they are not alert. They simply rest. Use it as your protection.

"Leo trusts you, and so do I. But please, forget this while you are there. Otherwise, it will be a burden too heavy for you to carry. You are not responsible for any of us. You're responsible only for yourself. Be true to yourself."

The Man paused for a moment and then continued. "I won't be able to help you, although I will be there. All the Shohonks will be there. You can't address me or talk to me. For three days, I will be a stranger. Please respect this. For these three days, you are on your own. Whatever you have built within yourself will be there for you. Go your way, and may Mother Nature's angels be with you, Tasha. Go now."

His voice was very calm and soft, yet he radiated strength and power. He had changed. He had regained his impressive presence. In that moment, the resemblance to Ian had reappeared, but she couldn't ask him any questions about this. It wasn't the right time.

"Good-bye, dear Man," she said. "Thank you for your kind words."

Tasha went back to the village. She collected her few things and asked her feet to take her to the place of the gathering. The day had come, and she was ready.

It took her a day to reach the place. It was in the center of the vast Nowhere. There were no signs, no directions. To access the place, she needed to enter another dimension, and she was surprised by how simple it was. There were no guardians to keep the gathering safe.

It was early in the morning on the first day of the gathering. Some Shohonks were already there, so she became transparent. She remembered what the Man had said: "When Shohonks feel safe, they are not alert." Tasha knew that she couldn't remain transparent for all three days. At the right time, she would take the shape of a Shohonk to enable her to blend in with the others.

They were all dressed in gowns of brown, orange, yellow, and red. Warm colors, colors of the sun. Then she understood that each realm had its own color: yellow for the East, brown for the

South, red for the North, and orange for the West. Each realm sat in different areas, according to the four winds.

The people she saw were happy and pleased to see each other again. They didn't leave their own areas, although they spoke to people from other areas. Some of them spoke through words. But most of them spoke through silence, nodding their heads with full understanding.

Tasha couldn't see the higher ranks of Shohonks there. It was still the early hours of the first day, and the gathering had just started. Children and adults continued to enter the dimension and silently go to their areas in the ceremony place. The atmosphere was light and free, although the order was impeccable. She heard people talking, and the word *persecution* repeated itself, but Tasha couldn't sense fear. It was as if the gathering gave the people a sense of strength and security.

As Tasha looked at the faces of the people in the East section, she saw Tia and Ethan. They were so fragile and vulnerable, like small children. It was as if they let themselves be unarmed under the inspiration of their powerful masters. Many of the young adults had this innocent look. They were still the children who had been taken from their parents.

Then silence was everywhere, as the junior masters of the realms entered. They were in their thirties and forties. They trained the people to become true Shohonks. Most of them were men, but Tasha saw a few women in the group. The children and adults adored the masters. Tasha sensed it in the air. She looked at their faces and saw Lee among them. He belonged to the realm of the East. She wasn't surprised. He had been there for her, guiding and teaching her how to face her past, and she thanked him in her heart for that.

After the entrance of the junior masters, the higher ranks of masters entered. There were eight of them, two for each realm. She recognized the two elders from the East realm she had seen before. But she was surprised to see Elijah standing there in the realm of the South, in the realm of Ceyon. She was the only woman who had reached this higher rank. Above them were only the four Masters.

Tasha chose not to stay sitting among the Shohonks in the opening of the first day. It was too quiet, too sacred. She wasn't one of them, and she knew it. There was a great danger of being identified, even by sitting there, so she looked for a hideaway. The ceremony took place in a small valley, surrounded by hills and forests. It was quite easy for her to find a safe shelter and still witness the ceremony. All the Shohonks were sitting, except for the eight masters.

Then one of the masters of the West said, "Dear Shohonks, the gathering opens now. We must try to leave this gathering wiser than we are now, kinder than we are now, stronger than we are now. These are days of elevation. Let us face them with great care and love. We have all been granted the gift of clear sight. Let us make it clearer. Let us take it to unimaginable frontiers. Let us be true Shohonks, tomorrow as well as today. The gathering opens now. Let us begin."

His words brought festive winds. Tasha could sense happiness and joy penetrating her heart.

One of the masters of the North said, "We'll give you knowledge to enrich you, to make you wiser. Don't become attached to this knowledge, however. Just absorb it with all your being. Remember, dear Shohonks, knowledge can lift your spirit, but will never *be* your spirit."

Then Elijah said, "We will show you how to perform miracles. You'll be amazed by your powers. But, remember, the use of the power determines who you are. Without a heart, the power is meaningless. So don't forget your hearts."

One of the masters of the East said, "Come, dear people, let us give this gathering a dignified shape and an honest form. Let us aspire to create a world that can bring the end of suffering, agony, and fear. We, who have the ability to see, have a great responsibility for this world. Let us turn this gathering, in our prayers and thoughts, into a real opportunity for all of us and for all the people of the world."

And finally, after the four speeches, a young boy stood in the center and sang an angelic song. His voice was high and pure. His song was touched by sanctity and sacred spirits. Tasha felt it, and it was beautiful. She looked at the people who had gathered to celebrate the beautiful side of their world, yet without the courage to also see their own shadows, Tasha knew that the gathering remained a mere facade.

After the song was over, the Shohonks of the four realms departed. The gathering had begun. And it had begun for Tasha as well.

61. ONLY PURE WILL

No Limits, No Constraints, No Borders

At twilight, the Shohonks gathered again in the ceremony place. Tasha couldn't see the Man and assumed he wasn't there.

A man in a white gown stood in the center and said, "This is the time to learn about transformation. Day will be transformed into night; warmth will be transformed into cold. And for a moment, your wishes are going to be transformed into real experiences. Now, see in your mind's eyes your deepest will. Take your time. Don't let whims penetrate your kingdom. Only pure will, your will, is about to blossom. This is your chance, dear people, to envision who you want to be, and for this night, to be it. Only for this night. When you wake up tomorrow, you'll have only a memory, nothing more. Yet, from then on, do whatever you can to live this memory. Then it will be yours. Tonight you have the chance to touch your sacred place. Give yourself this chance, and we will all serve you in this great mission.

"Now, take your time, and see your deepest will." Then he stopped speaking, and silence was everywhere.

Tasha wanted to touch her deepest will as well. She wanted to give herself the chance to live this will for the next few hours. *The one who touches his will can never be detached from it again,* she thought. So she took the shape of a Shohonk and joined the ceremony.

After a while, the man in the white gown continued his speech. "Now after each of you has seen his deepest will, it's time for experience. We will cross the dimension of time and space. You will taste a different world, but only for these moments. Don't be afraid. We are here to protect you. You don't have to know what you are going to experience. All you have to know is your deepest will."

Then he asked them to close their eyes and warned them not to open them until the experience was over. "Your will needs time to establish itself properly in your heart. Otherwise, it can be twisted," he said to them. "Be careful, and follow my directions."

Tasha closed her eyes. She saw her deepest wish: to be a leader of a new world. But she wasn't alone. She saw Ian with her. Then she heard an inner voice saying, *You can't do it alone. You must do it together.* She wanted to open her eyes, but didn't. She trusted the man in the white gown and followed his words.

Then her body started to shake. It was a gentle shaking, yet nothing remained stable. She became older. She felt that she had lived many years. Her body was filled with love. There was no trace of fear. Her passion was transformed into wisdom. She was free. She was flying. There were no limits, no constraints, no borders. She became endless. And there was Ian. He was different, yet the same. The color of his freedom was different from hers. His wings were different from hers, but he was free as well. She felt great joy, but she also felt great responsibility. Then she saw many people around them, thousands of people, and recalled Lynn's words: "You are filled with love, young woman. Go and give it." The world became small yet endless, friendly yet not intimate. She looked at Ian and felt that each of them had chosen their ways. Their ways were not different; they were the same. They were one. Then she experienced another shaking throughout her body, and the vision stopped.

Tasha didn't open her eyes. She waited for the man in the white gown to speak. Her vision had seemed so real, yet maybe it had been only her fantasy. Suddenly, her experience disappeared. Not even one grain was left. Her doubts had banished her vision.

She stayed there, feeling empty. She thought about the Shohonks sitting next to her. *Have they experienced the same thing as me?* she asked herself. *Do they have doubts that consumed their dreams, as mine did?*

She didn't want to open her eyes. She respected the rules of the ceremony, although she wanted to know what was happening around her. She was curious to see the other Shohonks, how they faced their visions. So she eventually opened her eyes.

Silence was everywhere. The Shohonks sat without a single movement. They were on their own journeys, and it was an amazing sight. No one opened his or her eyes. It was beautiful, but Tasha saw the shadow of it. It was more than respect for the rules. She saw the obedience, and she saw the seclusion. *They can't change the world,* she thought. *They are secluded in their intimate world. They have their own language, their own rituals, their own codes. They are not able to reach other people's hearts. And without the heart, as Elijah had said, the power is meaningless.*

Tasha left the ceremony place. She couldn't stay any longer. She didn't belong to the Shohonks. If, for a moment, she had thought differently, it had been nothing but an illusion, a fantasy.

She went back to her hideaway. The first day of the gathering had reached its end. There were two days before her, and that was not much time.

62. THE SCREEN

Paradise Can Turn Into Hell

The second day of the gathering arrived, and the Man still wasn't there. Tasha hadn't seen him. It was a riddle. She hoped he was safe. *Who keeps the guardians?* she asked herself. *Who guards him?*

The morning was fresh, and the Shohonks were already awake. *Did they meet their deepest wills? Did they touch them? Did they take a memory with them to lead them in the days to come?*

The ceremony place was empty, except for the man in the white gown standing in the middle, as if meditating. The Shohonks waiting outside seemed to have great respect for him and were silent. After a while, they entered and sat down.

The man in the center said, "Now is the time for you to show us who you are. I'll call your masters to come and enjoy your performances. Let the masters come in."

And then the eight masters entered the place. They sat on a high stage in a row, ready to see their people. Their beauty and strength were visible, and the Shohonks looked at them with great admiration and love. These eight masters were their parents, their teachers, their family.

The man in the white gown then joined the eight masters and said, "Let the West realm begin. Show us who you are."

The junior masters, who stood behind their people, started the show. One of them said, "We, the people of the West, want to show you the Power of the Word. Let the show begin."

Above the heads of the Shohonks from the West a large screen appeared. Tasha saw how the Shohonks from the West projected beams from their heads. Although each beam was sharp and thin, all the beams together created a full and wide screen.

The junior master continued, "This screen can reflect your will. Without a clear will, you won't be able to use the Power of the Word correctly. You'll be asked to articulate your will into words that capture the essence of it. If your will is vague or uncertain, the reflection will project this vagueness. But if your will is clear and precise, the projection will be clear and precise as well, and you will be able to see what your will is. If you have a strong desire, clear and precise, and you mistakenly think that it is your deep will, however, the screen will become black. The kingdom of darkness will be its projection."

The screen turned toward the Shohonks of the East, and the junior master said to them, "Shohonks of the East, each of you, look at this screen. You will be able to see only your personal projection. The screen knows how to protect your privacy. Articulate your deep will, and then look at the screen and see the reflection of it."

Tasha saw that all of the Shohonks from the East waited for a while, as if trying to put their wills into words. Then they looked at the screen. Some of them remained serious. Some of them laughed with joy. They saw their reflection. Tasha, who was hidden behind the East section, was tempted to look at the screen, too. *If the screen projects my will from last night, I will know that I am not trapped in a fantasy. It's a powerful tool to help people see what their real wills are.* Because of the privacy, she felt safe enough, so she looked at the screen. She saw darkness. The screen had turned black. *Am I so far from my deep will?* she asked herself.

Suddenly, she saw Lee turning around sharply toward her. He looked straight at her. Although he was far from her, she saw his eyes. His look conveyed a warning, as if saying, *Don't participate in this. Otherwise, your will might be in great danger.* He had turned around for only a moment, but it was enough. She knew that Lee had protected her, preventing her projection reaching the screen, and that explained the darkness she had seen.

After a while, the screen was turned to the south and then to the north. When the round was completed, the screen disappeared.

At that point, the junior master said, "This is our gift to the Shohonk people. Without following your deepest will, you won't be able to be free. Sometimes, the voices from within speak so loudly, we can't hear our deepest will. We hope that this screen will serve all of us in a good way, helping us all to be clear in our hearts and minds."

He sat down, and the other junior masters from the West sat down with him.

Tasha knew that this day would be long. Each realm would bring its gift to the service of the Shohonks. She couldn't stop thinking about the Man, however, and decided to leave the dimension to look for him.

She went out of the dimension quite easily. She found herself back in the endless meadows, where there were no signs or directions. She asked her feet to take her to the Man.

To her surprise, they took her to the gates of Lovelle. She waited by the gates, asking the Man to meet her there. But he didn't arrive. She wanted to find him, so she called him again. And finally, he came.

He stood there and said, "I told you that for these three days, I wouldn't be there for you. You must not call me."

"Where were you?" Tasha asked.

"I was here and there," he answered. "There is only a day before the meeting. You can't think about me. I'm not part of it. You are on your own. Your thoughts are merely a distraction. Be vacant. Be free of fear. Do you understand me?"

He wasn't gentle, but he was filled with love.

"Why Lovelle?" she asked him.

"Remember, Tasha," he answered. "Paradise can turn into hell. Don't trust the appearance. I must go. Don't call me, no matter what happens. When you call me, everyone can hear. Good-bye, Tasha. Follow your will."

Paradise can turn into hell, Tasha thought to herself. *Is the beautiful outward appearance of the Shohonks part of it?*

When she tried to enter the dimension of the Shohonks again, the entrance had disappeared.

What has happened? she asked herself.

She tried in different ways to enter the dimension, but she couldn't get through. She was left outside. She couldn't call the Man, and no one was there to help her. She didn't know what to do. She couldn't even look at the shadow of the entrance, because the entrance itself had disappeared.

She had to let go of these thoughts. Meeting the four Masters was what she really wanted to do. She remembered that the Masters' appearance would be at the end of the third day, so they had probably yet to enter the dimension. Tasha decided to wait for them. She didn't know when the Masters would arrive, but she knew that she couldn't miss them. She trusted Mother Nature and her angels to help her enter the dimension at the right time.

63. SHEER GREED

Voices, Steps, People

Morning came. It was the morning of the third day of the gathering. Once again Tasha tried to enter the dimension of the Shohonks, but the entrance still wasn't there, so she continued to wait.

A few hours passed before she heard voices, steps, and people. She stood where the entrance had been and became transparent. *When Shohonks feel safe,* she remembered, *they are not alert.*

Then she saw them. Each of the Masters wore simple clothing. They hadn't put on their gowns. They looked like ordinary people, although with a careful look, one could see their impressive presence. All four of them were tall, taller than most people. It was as if their height marked them. But then, to her surprise, she saw the Man. He followed the Masters. There were the four Masters and him.

He must be the closest person to them, Tasha thought. *He isn't as simple a person as I thought.*

The entrance reappeared, and Tasha stepped in without hesitation. She had to be the first to enter. She quickly moved to the side to let them pass through.

The ceremony place was empty. She couldn't see any Shohonks other than the four Masters and the Man.

They didn't speak with each other but used a sign language, which Tasha couldn't understand. Then each of the four Masters went in a different direction and disappeared. Only the Man remained. She felt tempted to talk with him, but she remembered his words: "When you call me, everyone can hear."

He must stay a stranger, she told herself.

The Man began to prepare the ceremony place. He arranged four stones to mark the four realms. Each stone was a different shape. He seemed very sure in his actions, as if this wasn't the first time he did this. His every movement was firm and accurate. There was no wasting of energy, no wandering about. He was a beautiful sight to see.

Tasha left the ceremony place. She wanted to know what the other Shohonks were doing, so she walked toward the area of the West. Although Leo had told her that the East had the power of protection, she wanted to see the people of the West, the Kingdom of the Word. She remembered that Emor was the strongest Master and thought that his people must be similar to him in spirit. When she looked at them, she was going to see Emor himself. So she went to the West.

On reaching the place, she witnessed a strange scene. The Shohonks of the West were watching the screen from yesterday and linking the wills that were reflected on the screen to the individual Shohonks. There had been no privacy at all. The words of the West realm had been false. They had played with words to create a false sense of trust, exploiting the innocence of the Shohonks of the other realms.

Tasha found a secure hideaway from where she could see and hear everything. They seemed to be classifying the other Shohonks by their wills, into three groups: friends, enemies, and the indifferent.

Friends were those who loved being Shohonks and admired their masters without doubt or question. Enemies were those with doubts. They might doubt their masters or their own paths, and these doubts were considered dangerous. The indifferent were people who didn't really care—they merely functioned. They had neither great admiration nor doubts.

Tasha looked at the Shohonks from the West as they fulfilled their assignment. They respected and obeyed their masters. Although they had been gifted with clear sight, they were too naïve to see that someone wanted them to remain blind. It was a devastating misuse of power. The gathering was supposed to be sacred. It was supposed to be an elevation, a transformation, and yet sheer greed for power was present as well.

64. MOMENTS
OF INSPIRATION

Too Clear, Too Blunt

Night fell. The gathering was reaching its climax. The Shohonks of the four realms were already seated. The masters and the junior masters were standing behind their realms, as if backing up their people. The man in the white gown stood in the center, and the evening began.

"Dear Shohonks," he said, "we've reached the end of the gathering. The four Masters, our Masters, are about to enter the place. You've done your best through the last days, and each of you has a brighter image of yourself. Now is the time to watch the highest images of all, the four Masters. Look at them, watch them carefully, and may their performance be a moment of inspiration for all of us. Let the Masters come in, and let us all enjoy their utmost beauty." Then he stood aside, leaving the center vacant for the four Masters.

The first Master to come was Kedem, Master of the Kingdom of Shape and Form, Master of the East. He stood in the center and, suddenly, he became a fortress. Then he turned into a waterfall. He became a tree, a storm, lightning. It was spectacular. Finally, he returned to his original shape. He stood there and didn't say a word.

His face was very kind, yet it conveyed power and strength. His eyes were innocent, but Tasha could see great pain in them. It was as if he saw things but couldn't act to make them different. Tasha looked at his side to see his shadow and saw his parents. They were still there. They were still his shadow. He was free and imprisoned at the same time. And he could see it. Tasha sensed this very clearly. He wasn't blind at all. He stood there quietly, radiating dignity and nobility. Then he walked to the back of his realm and stood behind the masters.

Next Tor, Master of the North, entered the place and stood in the center. Soon, a rain of wisdom started to pour upon the Shohonks. Each Shohonk received the unique drop of wisdom that he needed in his life. There was so much joy in the place. And then, in front of each Shohonk, a unique flower magically emerged from the earth. So many colors. So many flowers. It was a wonderful sight.

"Pick the flower," Tor said. "It is for you. The good earth and the good rain give you all the knowledge you need. Thank Mother Nature for all she brings you, but don't forget to be true friends to each other. Mother Nature can't give you that."

He stood there silently and didn't say another word. The appearance of Tor, the Master of the Kingdom of Knowledge, was very impressive. His eyes were fearless, yet Tasha could see the greed in them. When she looked at his side, she heard the word *more*. This was his shadow. He wanted more—more information and more knowledge. Yes, he was very curious, but it seemed that his curiosity didn't know where to stop. It was a startling feeling. She saw the admiration for him, and she sensed he enjoyed it. He walked to the back of his people, behind the masters, leaving the place in the center for the next Master.

Ceyon was next. Tasha felt deep love when she saw him. He stood in the center and didn't say a word. He just stood there not doing anything.

Then, suddenly, everything changed, everyone changed. The place turned into a large stadium. The seats were carved from stone. All the Shohonks were dressed in white gowns. There were no differences between the realms. Ceyon was still in the center, but he had become the conductor of an orchestra, and some of the Shohonks from his realm had become the musicians. Ceyon gave a sign to the orchestra, and they started to play beautiful music that combined different styles and textures. Ceyon was a passionate conductor and took his orchestra to a new realm of music. It was an unimaginable improvisation, yet it was also well structured. Beauty was in each note.

Yes, Tasha thought, *Ceyon was a wonder when he was a child. And he still is a wonder.*

When the music reached its end, the Shohonks applauded. Tasha saw the pride in Ceyon. He loved the sound of applause. He was worthy of it, yet too attached to it. The pride was still there, and the wonder was there as well.

Everything then returned to the way it had been before this wonderful experience. The Shohonks were dressed in their original gowns. The stadium disappeared. Ceyon stood in the center and didn't say anything.

What a sight, Tasha thought.

Ceyon walked to the back of his realm and stood behind the masters.

Then entered Emor, Master of the West, Master of the Word. He stood in the center. Like the other Masters, he was very impressive, but all innocence had disappeared from his eyes. Tasha couldn't see mercy in him. It was as if his desires had already conquered him.

Emor stood there for a while. Suddenly, Tasha saw some Shohonks burst into laughter. Then some other Shohonks burst into laughter, followed by another group. Emor must have done something, but Tasha didn't understand what.

He is certainly a master of secrets, Tasha thought. And his performance had the same quality.

Emor didn't do anything on the surface, yet all the Shohonks reacted to him very strongly. They clapped their hands, they sang, and they recited some words. They were amazed by him. He knew how to create this magic wisely and well. It was more like the performance of a master to his subjects, rather than a master to his people.

Tasha thought about the other Masters. *They must see what I can see,* she said to herself. *It's too clear. Too blunt.* The strongest master of all was playing with people's minds and hearts.

Then, silence returned to the place. Emor stood there surrounded by great admiration. Although Tasha watched the other Masters, she wasn't able to know what their thoughts were.

Emor went to the back of his realm and stood behind the masters. His eyes were pleased, too pleased. In a way, he had become blind.

Tasha expected the Shohonk in the white gown to enter, but to her surprise, the Man walked into the place. He didn't wear a gown, just simple clothing.

He stood in the center and said, "Dear Shohonks, remember who you are. Don't try to be who you are not. We were born to see. We were not born to lead. We are facing dire times, yet we were born only to see." Then he suddenly stopped speaking.

Tasha heard whispers among the Shohonks. No one had expected him to stop, but she knew that the Man had given her a signal. This was her sign to enter the place.

65. LEADER OF A NEW WORLD

No Secrets to Hide

Tasha entered the ceremony place. Silently and slowly she walked toward the center. The Shohonk people, as well as their masters, were astounded that she, a non-Shohonk, had been among them without them knowing it. She didn't wear a gown; she wore simple clothing. But her beauty was present, and she radiated grace and strength. She stood in the center without moving or saying a word. She stood with her back to the east and her face to the west. She knew that the people of the East would protect her.

She said, "Dear people of the Shohonks, I am not a Shohonk. I was not granted your powers, but I can see. I see your beauty, and it is a wonderful sight. As you all know, however, where there is beauty, a shadow also lurks. This gathering is a ceremony of beauty, but without seeing the shadows as well, one would not be able to see clearly."

Tasha turned around and looked at Lee. He didn't move but seemed to be there for her.

"You, the Shohonks, are unique," Tasha continued. "You are trained to give love without any attachment, but as you have experienced, it is not a simple task. Greed, shame, and pride lurk in all of us. We are all people. I know that I'm not one of *your* people," Tasha said, looking at Ceyon, "but aren't the words *our people* a sign of attachment?"

She looked at Elijah and said, "I came for a different journey. If you can see through me, you'll see that. I was fortunate to meet some of you on my journey. I was fortunate to see some of you in your spectacular moments, but life is made of many kinds of moments, not merely the beautiful ones. You all must know that."

She paused and then added, "Now I must talk to the four Masters alone, only them and me."

Tasha stood in the center and waited. She looked into Emor's eyes. She knew that if he looked at her, he wouldn't be able to say no to her request. Her deep will was being manifested. People who were trained to see couldn't ignore it.

Emor gave her a sign as if to say, "Follow me." Tasha left the ceremony place, following Emor. Ceyon, Kedem, and Tor didn't join them. It was only Emor and Tasha. She had wanted to talk with all four of them, but she knew that she must face reality as it is.

Emor stopped walking, turned, and looked at her very carefully. Tasha didn't put up a veil. A naked heart and bare hands were all she had. She looked at Emor and saw empty eyes—there were no impressions in them. Then she started to hear inner voices: *You are an intruder. You are a stranger. You don't belong here.* She understood what Emor had done in the ceremony: He had planted words in the Shohonks' minds. Perhaps not only words. Maybe he knew how to plant thoughts or emotions, as well.

Tasha didn't listen to the voices. She remembered Leo, who had reminded her to trust herself. "You are definitely worthy of trust," he had said.

She knew that Emor should say the first word, so she remained silent. The voices kept coming, but Tasha didn't react to them. They couldn't penetrate her heart. The voices grew stronger and stronger, and the content was harsher: *You are a danger to the Shohonks. You are a menace to all of us.*

Tasha looked at Emor's side and saw a young boy playing with a ball in a field. It was the same boy that she had seen in the eyes of Ceyon and the Man. While the boy was playing, she heard a loud argument between Emor and Ceyon.

"Don't touch this boy," Ceyon said.

"One day he will come after us," Emor replied. "He will be a great danger to us."

"Don't touch him," Ceyon insisted.

"The Shohonk people are my main responsibility," Emor said.

Ceyon kept saying, "Don't touch the boy. If you want to take his brother, so be it. But don't touch this boy."

"One day," Emor said, "you will be sorry."

Ceyon didn't answer. Emor and Ceyon left the field, but the little boy had seen them and told his parents about the two men in the field. A few weeks later, the little boy lost his entire family; they were gone. The boy was Ian.

Then she heard Emor asking, "Who are you?"

"You know who I am," she answered looking straight at him. "I have no secrets to hide."

"What do you want?"

"Stop taking children without their parents' consent. It leads to hatred and eliminates the chance for free spirits to emerge."

Emor didn't say a word. His face was like a blank page. "Who let you in?"

"Mother Nature and her good angels," Tasha replied.

"You are not one of us," he said.

"I am not a Shohonk, but I am a human being."

"This gathering is sacred, and you have violated it."

"No, I haven't. My words give you a true chance to bring sacredness back to the Shohonk realm. You are strong and immense, but the people outside think of you—of all of you—as a phantom. Trying to protect yourselves, you became more reclusive and more secretive. This has endangered you. How can people be your friends without seeing your faces, without hearing your voices, without addressing you by name? Slowly you have become monsters. Decent people can't afford to live with monsters. Help the people outside know the Shohonks. Otherwise, the results will be devastating, and you know it."

225

"I've heard your words. Now go. You can't stay here any longer. Leave our dimension."

"There is no *your* dimension or *our* dimension," Tasha replied. "If your dimension is haunting our dimension, we are in the same dimension, aren't we? You have brave people here. Don't mislead them."

Tasha looked straight into Emor's eyes. She was looking for a crack, a slit, an opening, even a narrow one. Yet the screen of blindness remained firm and steady. Emor was silent, and his eyes were dark. Nevertheless, Tasha decided to say what was in her mind and heart. *If Emor cannot hear me,* Tasha thought, *perhaps there are other Shohonks who can hear me out, even from a distance. I'm going to speak through Emor rather than with him. I would speak my heart out loud, out in the open, and trust that my yearning is not a private one. There are friends out there. There must be.*

Tasha took a step forward toward Emor and said, "I came here to the gathering trusting the clear sight of the four of you. Despite the shadows, I trusted that the years of training and being the Masters of the Shohonks would enable all of you to transcend pride and reclusiveness. I believe that truth is always your aim, and so is freedom.

"The abduction of children leads to suffering and hatred. It consumes people's hopes and aspirations. I care about people, and I care about their spirits. I want to help, for I can hear their cry. And whoever hears the cry must step forward, for he might be the only one to speak out.

"Today you might have the power, but don't underestimate the power of a sincere and honest heart. I trust that the realm of the Shohonks one day will rise again from its shadow, for clear sight is the essence of who you are."

And with those words, Tasha left the place. She walked straight to the entrance and didn't wait to hear Emor's response.

When she reached the entrance, the Man was there waiting for her.

"Thank you," she said, walking away.

"Tasha, stop," he said. "You have seen many things in the last three days. You've met the four Masters, and they've met you. You've also met another side of me. Remember your deep will. You didn't reach the end of it—you are only at the beginning. If you really want to be a leader of a new world, you can't do it alone."

Tasha had many questions to ask him, but it wasn't the time. She looked at him with much love and then walked through the entrance back to the real world, back to real life.

Tasha didn't know where to go or what to do. For the last months, she prepared herself for a grand meeting, but nothing was grand or glorious. To her surprise, she didn't feel empty or disappointed. In herself, she found deep silence.

Suddenly, she heard a voice from the outside, saying, "Great things come in silence."

She said, "I was willing to challenge my perceptions of what is possible, to create true change. Trusting that we are all people and words can create change."

"If you truly want to create that change," the voice replied, "know that there is only one question for you right now: What would you do tomorrow and in the days to come? Would you give up, or would you continue?"

"I . . . " Tasha started to answer.

"You don't need to answer," the voice said. "Your deeds will show where your heart is."

Tasha remained silent. The gathering had reached its end, but for her it was only a beginning, a new beginning.

66. GREAT DEEDS, GREAT LOVE

The Land Is Big

Tasha asked her feet to take her to her next destination, and after a few days, she reached the gates of Belle. Her feet didn't take her into the town, though; they stopped next to the gates. Tasha sat there and waited. She didn't know for whom or for what. All she did was sit and wait.

Soon, she heard a voice. "Hello, Tasha."

It was the Man. She turned around, and there he was. Tasha looked at him. He was peaceful and quiet.

"Hello," she said.

"How are you?" the Man asked as he sat down beside her.

"I don't really know yet," she replied. Then she continued, "I've seen Emor's shadow, and I've seen Ian in it. Can you tell me the full story of Ian, of Ceyon, and of yourself?"

The Man looked at her and said, "Tasha, I am not the right person to tell you this story. If you really want to know the truth, you must ask Ceyon for the full story."

"Why can't you tell me yourself?" Tasha asked.

"Please don't ask me why," the Man replied. "Just trust me. Go to Ceyon, Tasha. Go and talk to him. I must leave now. Take care of yourself." And he left.

Tasha remained sitting there and asked Ceyon to join her. "I don't know where I can find you, but I don't want to wander around anymore. Dear Ceyon, I'm here at the gates of Belle, as you know by now. Please come and meet me."

Night fell. Ceyon hadn't arrived, and Tasha stayed at the gates. She could go to Lynn's house, but she didn't want to leave the gates.

I'll stay here, she said to herself, *until Ceyon arrives.*

The morning came but Ceyon didn't, and Tasha didn't leave the place. She simply waited.

The following morning, she went to Lynn's house. Lynn was there and was happy to see her. She saw Tasha's beauty and her strength, yet she still saw pain in her.

"Dear Tasha," she said, "come in."

Lynn didn't ask her any questions, and in her heart, Tasha thanked her for that.

After a while, they heard a knock on the door. Lynn went to the door and asked the person to come in. "You have a visitor," she told Tasha.

When Tasha went to the front door, she saw Ceyon. She saw his kind eyes, and there was no trace of vanity or pride in them.

Lynn said, "I'll leave you two alone for a while." And she went out, closing the door behind her.

"Why didn't you come to the gates?" Tasha asked Ceyon after they sat down.

"Because I couldn't. The gates weren't safe."

"Ceyon . . ."

But Ceyon interrupted her gently, saying, "I know what you want. I owe you the full story, and I'm going to tell it to you. Please don't ask any questions." Then he paused for a moment. "Ian was marked at his birth to take a crucial role in leading the change toward a new world. Emor knew that, and didn't like it. Deep in his heart, he wants to form the new world in the image of his grand vision: The Shohonks will have immense powers and final say in creating the frontiers for humanity, and all will follow them with great appreciation and admiration. Therefore, Emor wanted to prevent Ian from fulfilling his destiny.

"Since Ian was a real chance for a new world, I couldn't let him do it. So Emor took Ian's brother, Luke, although he wasn't born to be a Shohonk. He thought that if Ian's brother was one of the Shohonks, his vision would be safe. Luke was taken when Ian was very small, and he was raised differently. Rather than being trained to become a Shohonk, he was raised to serve the four Masters. However, he was bright enough to decipher the codes and turn himself into a real Shohonk. Emor planned that Luke would be the one to stop Ian, if needed, at the right time. As you can imagine, Luke could see this, and it caused him great pain. Luke, Ian's brother, as you may know by now, is the Man." Then Ceyon stopped talking.

Tasha saw shame in his eyes, as if saying, *By letting Emor take Ian's brother, I wasn't very different from Emor.*

This vulnerable moment encouraged Tasha to ask the question that was left open. She looked at Ceyon and asked, "What happened on *that day* between us? We have never spoken about it, yet I wish to know: Did you truly give up on me *that day?* You told me once that my life was sacred. What changed it?"

Ceyon was quiet for a while. There were no remains of the struggle that was once there. Then he looked at Tasha and said, "Tasha, your life was sacred then as it is now. Nothing has changed. The first time I saw you, I knew you came for a different journey. I knew you must be well guarded.

"*That day* was crucial to the lives of the many Shohonks. And although I trusted that you'd be safe and well, my decision to leave your life in the hands of Mother Nature's angels cannot be justified."

Ceyon became quiet. It seemed as if he relived the moment of his decision and felt deep sorrow. Tasha could see the remorse in his eyes.

After a long moment Ceyon continued, saying, "I'm glad to see you have transcended all that, and I was glad to see you at the gathering, standing on your own feet, relying on your heart, without any fear or doubt, compelled by your sincere wish to create the change that you truly want."

"If I am a true chance to create this change," Tasha then said, "why did Emor look only for Ian and not for me?"

"You came to a different journey, Tasha. Your sincere and bold wish to be free marked your destiny. It was as if you came to this life with a sacred promise: As long as you are brave enough to be free, truly free in spirit and in deed, whatever you are wishing to accomplish will be possible for you to achieve.

"There are going to be challenges, yet your lack of hesitation to be free over and over again, despite the price, will grant you the ability to fulfill all that you truly wish for."

"Why did I get this promise?"

"Because there isn't enough free spirit on the face of the earth. It is your choice to be a leader of a new world that marks your future to come. It is your free will that has created it. This is why Emor couldn't foresee it, for a free spirit is always unpredictable."

"Do you trust that I can lead this change?" Tasha asked him.

"I know that you can. It is not a matter of trust. Your brave wish to seek true freedom within togetherness, within society, can touch people's hearts and lead to a genuine change. Yet you cannot do it alone. Therefore, go find Ian and govern the land, Tasha. Because the land is big, and great deeds and great love are needed. Only the two of you together can face this challenge.

"The era of a single individual who could change the world has come to an end. We are at the gates of a new era, the Era of Togetherness. Only through coming together will people be able to push human existence toward new realms and aspirations. Remember that, Tasha. Remember that especially in moments of testing, and it will keep your heart lucid and clear." Ceyon was quiet for a moment, as if knowing what the future concealed.

Then he said, "I can't stay here any longer."

"Before you leave," Tasha said, "have you seen the blindness in Emor's eyes?"

"Yes, I can see his shadow," Ceyon answered. "But the shadow of a leader is always a reflection of his people's shadows. If we remove Emor from his throne, the shadow will remain in the people's minds and hearts. Go, talk with the people, speak with their shadows, and let free spirits emerge. Take care of yourself, Tasha, and I will help you and Ian lead the change." And he went on his way.

Tasha thought about all that Ceyon had told her. She felt that now was the time to leave her past behind, along with the other questions she hadn't asked Ceyon. She heard the love and the trust in his words, yet she heard the warning in them as well. She remembered her inner voice saying, *You can't do it alone. You must do it together.* Luke, the Man, told her the same, and now Ceyon was saying, "Only the two of you together can face this challenge." Ceyon wouldn't ask her to remember these words, unless he had seen her forgetting them in the days to come. But she decided to leave that to the hands of life and move on.

Tasha knew what her next destination would be. It had a face and a name. It was Ian.

67. NOWHERE

Now and Here

Tasha reached the town and went straight to the empty house, Ian's old home. She didn't enter. She waited outside, asking Ian to join her. It was morning, and the air was fresh.

When she looked at the empty house, it seemed haunted, and she remembered that the Shohonks were often perceived as ghosts. Their touch created haunted houses and haunted people.

The story Ceyon had told her didn't leave her. She thought about Ian, about the Man, and about Ceyon and Emor. *So much pain, so much pride . . . and all for what?* She understood why Ceyon had said that Emor wasn't the enemy. *The enemy, indeed, lurks within us,* she thought. *Pride is a ruthless master. Nevertheless, it's not an excuse to be passive or indifferent.*

Then she heard a voice. "Hello, Tasha."

It was Ian. He sat down quietly next to her.

"How are you, Ian?"

"I'm fine. And you?"

Tasha laughed and said, "I'm fine, too. Did you meet your brother?"

"Yes, I did. And he sent me back to you."

She looked at him and asked, "What did he say?"

"He said that he couldn't tell me the full story. If I wanted the truth, I had to ask you."

Tasha smiled. *Dear Man,* she said to herself, *you are clever. You've sent me to Ceyon for the truth, and now you've sent Ian to me for his truth.*

Tasha told Ian the full story about *that day* of his, as Ian sat silently and listened. He didn't move. After she finished the story, she looked at him.

Ian remained silent, as if he needed time to grasp everything. Then he looked at Tasha and asked, "And what is your *that day,* Tasha? What was haunting you?"

Tasha didn't expect his question, but she didn't hesitate; she wanted to tell Ian her story. Yet first, she took some time to be in touch again with the flow of events, with the stream of her life.

After a short while, she told Ian about *that day* in the mud, followed by all that had happened, until the very last conversation with Ceyon. She spoke slowly and chose her words with care and love. It was the first time that she had revealed her story to Ian, and she wanted it to be told as it truly was.

Ian listened wholeheartedly as if it were his own story. He didn't interrupt or ask any questions. He just listened quietly until the story reached its end.

Then came silence. They sat there, just the two of them with the truth between them—the truth that had turned their *that day* into only a memory.

After letting their spirits rest, Tasha asked Ian, "Now that you know everything, are you going to speak with your brother about all that has happened?"

"It seems like the right thing to do," Ian answered. "But, no, I'm not going to speak about it with Luke. He chose you to tell me my story instead of him. I'm sure that he had his reasons, and I intend to respect that." Ian paused for a moment and then said, "Ceyon told you that he trusted you to lead the change. Are you ready to do so? Are you ready to reach the ocean?"

Tasha paused, and then said, "Yes, I am. But I can't do it alone."

"You are not alone. Look at me, Tasha—you are not alone."

When she looked into Ian's eyes, the ocean was there. It was her ocean and his. It was the same ocean.

"Let's go to Nowhere, Ian," she said. "Yet this time, let's go together."

"Tasha, a wise man once told me that when you dare to go to Nowhere, you have a real chance to meet Now and Here."

"That is beautiful," she said.

Ian looked at Tasha, and he loved what he saw. "There are great things ahead of you," he said to her.

Tasha looked back at him and smiled. "There are great things ahead of *us*."

EPILOGUE

Tasha was born with a single cry, yet her initiation ended in silence. The initiation of the one is a journey to one's inner depths, and so always ends in silence. You may think that the completion should be dramatic and glorious, but there aren't any exclamation marks at the end of this road. There is stillness rather than victory, quietness rather than festivity. *Humble, intimate, close to the heart—* these are the words you are about to meet. The time for victory will come, but not just yet.

The meeting between Tasha and the Masters at the gathering didn't stop the abductions, and hate and pain still surrounded the land. Yet Tasha's words echoed in the minds and hearts of the Shohonks who were seeking a change but not allowed to lead it. At the time, Tasha's deeds may have seemed in vain, but her bravery and genuine wish stamped their mark on our world. Sometimes there is a need for a stranger to help you find your hidden, innermost truths. And so was Tasha. A stranger, who taught us, the Shohonks, about ourselves and never gave up, even in dire times.

I, Ceyon, was her guardian, her teacher. I saw her beauty then, as I see it now. I gave my word to help her and Ian lead the change to a new world.

Little did they know that the new world they were heading toward would not be found, but was yet to be created. It would be formed by the deep hopes and aspirations of the many people they were about to lead through the gates of a new era.

I gave my word to help them, but life can be more complicated than that. And so it was.

We are only in the beginning of the story, of our story. There is much more to tell. Take care of yourselves, dear friends. When the time comes, we will meet again.

ABOUT THE AUTHOR

Ronit Galapo co-founded the Ronit Galapo Research Institute in 2003 with a desire to bring forth genuine change through pioneering research and cutting-edge technology. For the past 20 years, she has been engaged in the profound inquiry and deciphering of the underlying mechanisms shaping our lives, our illnesses, our health, our relationships, and society as a whole.

Ronit's research has led to a series of groundbreaking discoveries, based on which she developed innovative consciousness technologies that make it possible to effect change in areas thought to be blocked, such as autism. Over the years, Ronit has held lectures and seminars before large audiences, and has written six books. *Strong Winds from Nowhere* has been translated into seven languages across Europe and Japan.

Hay House Titles of Related Interest

YOU CAN HEAL YOUR LIFE, the movie, starring Louise Hay & Friends
(available as a 1-DVD program and an expanded 2-DVD set)
Watch the trailer at: www.LouiseHayMovie.com

THE SHIFT, the movie,
starring Dr. Wayne W. Dyer
(available as a 1-DVD program and an expanded 2-DVD set)
Watch the trailer at: www.DyerMovie.com

LINDEN'S LAST LIFE: The Point of No Return Is Just the Beginning,
by Alan Cohen

THE MAN WHO WANTED TO BE HAPPY, by Laurent Gounelle

PUSHING UPWARD, by Andrea Adler

SOLOMON'S ANGELS, by Doreen Virtue

THROUGH INDIGO'S EYES, by Tara Taylor and Lorna Schultz Nicholson

WAITING FOR AUTUMN, by Scott Blum

All of the above are available at your local bookstore,
or may be ordered by contacting Hay House (see next page).

We hope you enjoyed this Hay House Visions book. If you'd
like to receive our online catalog featuring additional information
on Hay House books and products, or if you'd like to find out
more about the Hay Foundation, please contact:

Hay House, Inc., P.O. Box 5100, Carlsbad, CA 92018-5100
(760) 431-7695 or (800) 654-5126
(760) 431-6948 (fax) or (800) 650-5115 (fax)
www.hayhouse.com® • www.hayfoundation.org

Published and distributed in Australia by: Hay House Australia Pty. Ltd.,
18/36 Ralph St., Alexandria NSW 2015 • *Phone:* 612-9669-4299
Fax: 612-9669-4144 • www.hayhouse.com.au

Published and distributed in the United Kingdom by: Hay House UK, Ltd.,
Astley House, 33 Notting Hill Gate, London W11 3JQ • *Phone:* 44-20-3675-2450
Fax: 44-20-3675-2451 • www.hayhouse.co.uk

Published and distributed in the Republic of South Africa by: Hay House SA
(Pty), Ltd., P.O. Box 990, Witkoppen 2068 • *Phone/Fax:* 27-11-467-8904
www.hayhouse.co.za

Published in India by: Hay House Publishers India, Muskaan Complex, Plot No.
3, B-2, Vasant Kunj, New Delhi 110 070 • *Phone:* 91-11-4176-1620
Fax: 91-11-4176-1630 • www.hayhouse.co.in

Distributed in Canada by: Raincoast Books, 2440 Viking Way,
Richmond, B.C. V6V 1N2 • *Phone:* 1-800-663-5714 • *Fax:* 1-800-565-3770
www.raincoast.com

Take Your Soul on a Vacation

Visit www.HealYourLife.com® to regroup, recharge,
and reconnect with your own magnificence.
Featuring blogs, mind-body-spirit news, and life-changing
wisdom from Louise Hay and friends.

Visit www.HealYourLife.com today!

Free e-newsletters from Hay House, the Ultimate Resource for Inspiration

Be the first to know about Hay House's dollar deals, free downloads, special offers, affirmation cards, giveaways, contests, and more!

 Get exclusive excerpts from our latest releases and videos from *Hay House Present Moments*.

 Enjoy uplifting personal stories, how-to articles, and healing advice, along with videos and empowering quotes, within *Heal Your Life*.

 Have an inspirational story to tell and a passion for writing? Sharpen your writing skills with insider tips from *Your Writing Life*.

Sign Up Now!

Get inspired, educate yourself, get a complimentary gift, and share the wisdom!

http://www.hayhouse.com/newsletters.php

Visit www.hayhouse.com to sign up today!

 HAY HOUSE

 HAYHOUSE RADIO® *radio for your soul*®

HealYourLife.com

Heal Your Life One Thought at a Time . . .
on Louise's All-New Website!

"Life is bringing me everything
I need and more."

— Louise Hay

Come to HEALYOURLIFE.COM today and meet the world's best-selling self-help authors; the most popular leading intuitive, health, and success experts; up-and-coming inspirational writers; and new like-minded friends who will share their insights, experiences, personal stories, and wisdom so you can heal your life and the world around you . . . one thought at a time.

Here are just some of the things you'll get at HealYourLife.com:

- DAILY AFFIRMATIONS
- CAPTIVATING VIDEO CLIPS
- EXCLUSIVE BOOK REVIEWS
- AUTHOR BLOGS
- LIVE TWITTER AND FACEBOOK FEEDS
- BEHIND-THE-SCENES SCOOPS
- LIVE STREAMING RADIO
- "MY LIFE" COMMUNITY OF FRIENDS

PLUS:
FREE Monthly Contests and Polls
FREE BONUS gifts, discounts,
and newsletters

Make It Your Home Page Today!
www.HealYourLife.com®

HEAL YOUR LIFE♥

Join the

HAY HOUSE
Family

As the leading self-help, mind,
body and spirit publisher in the UK,
we'd like to welcome you to our
community so that you can keep
updated with the latest news, including
new releases, exclusive offers,
author events and more.

Sign up at www.hayhouse.co.uk/register

**Like us on Facebook
at Hay House UK**

**Follow us on Twitter
@HayHouseUK**

www.hayhouse.co.uk

Hay House Publishers
Astley House, 33 Notting Hill Gate, London W11 3JQ
020 3675 2450   info@hayhouse.co.uk

Lightning Source UK Ltd.
Milton Keynes UK
UKOW07f2256041214

242637UK00008B/149/P